Pra

New York Times **and** *US.. ....., ...* **A**u**t**h**o**r

Diane Capri

"Full of thrills and tension, but smart and human, too."
Lee Child, #1 New York Times Bestselling Author of Jack Reacher Thrillers

"[A] welcome surprise....[W]orks from the first page to 'The End'."
Larry King

"Swift pacing and ongoing suspense are always present...[L]ikable protagonist who uses her political connections for a good cause...Readers should eagerly anticipate the next [book]."
Top Pick, Romantic Times

"...offers tense legal drama with courtroom overtones, twisty plot, and loads of Florida atmosphere. Recommended."
Library Journal

"[A] fast-paced legal thriller...energetic prose...an appealing heroine...clever and capable supporting cast...[that will] keep readers waiting for the next [book]."
Publishers Weekly

"Expertise shines on every page."
Margaret Maron, Edgar, Anthony, Agatha and Macavity Award Winning MWA Past President

FATAL
ACTION

by DIANE CAPRI

Published by: AugustBooks
http://www.AugustBooks.com

ISBN: 978-1-942633-66-2

Original Cover Design: Cory Clubb
Digital Formatting: Author E.M.S.

Published in the United States of America.

Visit the author website:
http://www.DianeCapri.com

BOOKS BY DIANE CAPRI

THE JESS KIMBALL THRILLERS:
Fatal Distraction
Fatal Demand
Fatal Error
Fatal Fall
Fatal Game
Fatal Bond
Fatal Enemy (*novella*)
Fatal Edge (*novella*)
Fatal Past (*novella*)
Fatal Heat (*novella*)
Fatal Dawn

THE HUNT FOR JACK REACHER SERIES:
(in publication order with Lee Child source books in parentheses)
Don't Know Jack • (Killing Floor)
Jack in a Box (*novella*)
Jack and Kill (*novella*)
Get Back Jack • (Bad Luck and Trouble)
Jack and Joe • (The Enemy)
Deep Cover Jack • (Persuader)
Jack in the Green (*novella*)
Jack the Reaper • (The Hard Way)
Black Jack • (Running Blind / The Visitor)
Ten Two Jack • (The Midnight Line)
Jack of Spades • (Past Tense)
Prepper Jack • (Die Trying)

Full Metal Jack • (The Affair)
Jack Frost • (61 Hours)
Jack of Hearts • (Worth Dying For)
Straight Jack • (A Wanted Man)
Jack Knife • (Never Go Back)

THE HUNT FOR JUSTICE SERIES:
Due Justice
Twisted Justice
Secret Justice
Wasted Justice
Raw Justice
Mistaken Justice (*novella*)
Cold Justice (*novella*)
False Justice (*novella*)
Fair Justice (*novella*)
True Justice (*novella*)
Night Justice

THE PARK HOTEL MYSTERIES:
Reservation with Death
Early Check Out
Room with a Clue
Late Arrival

FATAL
ACTION

CONTENTS

Fatal Enemy   11

Fatal Edge   49

Fatal Past   99

Fatal Heat   143

Jack in the Green   193

FATAL
ENEMY

For Robert

CHAPTER ONE

JESS KIMBALL SWITCHED THE Glock's grip to her left hand, raised her right to rub her sore neck and stretched her shoulders. Her body seemed to hum at the cellular level. She felt fatigued, yet buzzingly alert. She hadn't been in the same room with Richard Martin for more than a dozen years. Worse things than Richard had happened to her since she'd seen him last. He'd find out soon enough that she wasn't a gullible sixteen-year-old anymore.

Dressed crown to sole in black, sitting as still as the furniture, Jess was indistinguishable from her surroundings. Ambient light was non-existent in the quiet neighborhood, where *crime* should've been non-existent. The microwave clock glowed 3:00:15 a.m. providing the room's only illumination.

Jess leaned back, ankles crossed, heels propped on the kitchen table, and settled in to wait through the remainder of the third night. A bouquet of Stargazer lilies stood across the room but their fragrant perfume filled the air like oxygen. Richard was allergic to Stargazers. Jess appreciated the subtle torture although she hadn't planned it.

Man, she hated custody battles; the children always lose. But this custody dispute was different, more vital. She couldn't refuse to help this time because the victim was Richard Martin's daughter. Knowing Richard as she did would make the difference between success and failure.

As malevolent a bastard as ever drew breath, Richard was far from stupid. He would try to steal Anna until someone stopped him. If not tonight, then tomorrow or another night soon. Jess felt it, yes. Instinct and preparation had saved her life before. She wouldn't ignore them now. But hunches were not enough.

Her throat was parched, but she couldn't risk a trip to the faucet for water. Time seemed stagnant even as the clock reflected 3:10:21 a.m. Combating boredom, her thoughts wandered again to Richard when she'd been in lust with him. Inside the ski mask, her face burned now with a different heat. He'd been her first romance when she was sixteen and seeking love wherever she could find it. She'd felt as treasured as a rare art object for about three weeks. The warning signs were there if only she'd been sophisticated enough to recognize them. She wasn't. She'd made a significant mistake a long time ago, and it had defined her life evermore.

Undisclosed petty crimes and scandals had blown the Martin family into her town, and serious crimes hastened them away a year later. Richard had turned eighteen as his crimes escalated. He'd have gone to prison. A chill ran through her as she recalled how narrowly she'd escaped his bondage when Richard's parents rushed him to a new jurisdiction moments before his arrest for grand theft auto.

Jess stretched again, shifted the gun purposefully at 3:12:46 a.m. She noted its heft increasing with the slightest attention paid during the passing seconds. *Show yourself, Richard, you coward.*

Richard never knew that he'd left her pregnant with Peter. Nor had he cared. Jess's embarrassed adolescent pride kept the news from him at first. Later, when she realized his miserable domination for what it was, she concealed Peter from Richard and vowed she always would. Not that he'd ever looked back. Jess was grateful for that much.

She'd never told anyone who'd fathered her son. Nor would she. When people asked, she simply said she didn't know. If pressed for more details, she said she'd been raped by an unknown assailant who was never apprehended, which was technically accurate but not true. She'd been a minor back then and Richard was not, so what he'd done was statutory rape and he'd have gone to jail if anyone had bothered to report his crime. But she'd been a willing participant in his seduction. Still, "rape" described precisely how she felt when Richard tossed her aside like a used rag. Maybe that was when anger's spark lodged firmly in her gut and flamed whenever Richard's name was mentioned.

So far, the rape answer had sufficed. No one ever tried to hunt down a man Jess Kimball couldn't find for herself. People assumed an investigative journalist of her stature, coupled with her national crusade for victims' rights, made Jess infallible as a prison-trained bloodhound. Which was true.

3:23:07 a.m. How much longer should she wait tonight? At least until dawn. She'd promised Betsy. And then she'd be back tomorrow. Richard had told Betsy he was coming, simply to terrorize her further. Jess would be waiting for as long as it took.

Jess inhaled deeply, drawing the Stargazers' fragrance into her lungs and remembered how she'd watched Richard's life from afar. Memories heated her temper and chased away the last of the early morning chill. He'd cut a wide swathe through a long list of gullible girls and later, gullible women. None of them were foolish enough to deliver his child afterward, but each one bore invisible scars Jess could easily discern just the same.

Until seven years ago when Richard seized sexier, younger, naive, sensitive and fragile Betsy. She never stood a chance.

Jess had contacted Betsy back then, tried to warn her before she married him, but Betsy's inexperience prevailed. Thus began the destructive tango that led them all here.

All these years later, Jess felt grateful to have escaped Richard's cruelty but guilty, too. *Survivor guilt* was what the psychologists called it. Irrational perhaps, but real enough. She shrugged; she supposed Richard had to marry someone eventually. He wasn't a man who'd remain single forever and Jess couldn't save all the Betsys in the world. She prayed silently, *Just this one, please.*

Jess wagged her head back and forth and stretched her neck, attempting to push the fatigue and the memories away. But her stress had long ago settled into knots harder than obsidian. She needed to stand, walk out the tension, but she couldn't risk being discovered. Failure was not an option. Not this time. She tried to focus on something other than her screaming muscles.

She couldn't keep her gaze from the microwave clock. *Only 3:34:17 a.m. Would this night never end?*

Betsy had never asked why Jess agreed to help her and thus spared the lies. Betsy didn't know Richard had fathered a son or that Peter was kidnapped. Betsy presented Jess with a second chance to save Betsy and her daughter before Richard destroyed them as he'd destroyed Jess and Peter. Maybe Betsy had forgotten her worth, but Jess would not. Nor would she allow Richard to harm Peter's half-sister. Someday his sister's DNA would help Jess prove Peter's identity. When she found Peter, he'd have both his sister *and* his mother.

Jess avoided the ultimate question her son was sure to ask one day: "Why did you put my father in prison?"

At 3:54:17 a.m., as if her thoughts had conjured him, she heard Richard's heavy tread on the squeaky plank decking. Every nerve stood at attention while she remained as still as the lilies.

Jess pressed the remote button to activate the security camera outside the back door. The night vision would record every moment in an eerie green glow. She'd have the one thing she needed to nail the bastard—evidence.

She blended with the darkness and waited, holding the Glock in her right hand, ready to use it. But not too soon. Jess knew the law inside out. Only when Richard left the premises with Anna would he be guilty of kidnapping. Only then. Not a moment before.

Should she be forced to confront him earlier, he'd claim he wasn't taking Anna anywhere. A court would agree. Betsy was the custodial parent, but Richard had bought and still owned this house. Technically, he wasn't trespassing and he could visit whenever he chose. His twisted lies and intimidation had persuaded Betsy to excuse his behavior repeatedly.

Not this time. Jess would have irrefutable evidence and she'd use it effectively, just as she had when he stole that Jaguar all those years ago.

So Jess had to allow Richard to accomplish the crimes he'd come to commit instead of interrupting him in the act as Betsy had done twice before. Kidnapping would send him away for life, if there was any justice at all in the world.

But a just world would have locked Richard Martin up long ago before he raped Jess. A just world would never have taken Peter. The only just world Jess believed in was the one she created herself.

Watching the microwave clock, she timed him. Richard spent exactly twelve seconds forcing the lock and opening the back door. She smiled again. He should have tried his old key. She'd made sure it would work, just in case he proved less predictable than she'd expected. Overconfidence kills, that much she knew. But she knew him better than anyone else. Maybe better than he knew himself.

The security alarm began its incessant bleat the moment Richard opened the door. Jess breathed silently, disturbing the air as little as possible. He had the instincts of an apex predator at the top of the food chain and the top of his game. He would sense her presence if she made the slightest sound.

He crossed the tile to the alarm panel next to the refrigerator. He rapid-punched the six numbers of his wedding date, the code he and Betsy had chosen when he still lived here. Before their bitter divorce.

The alarm stopped well within the window of acceptable Miami PD response time.

He turned toward the next goal of his mission, never glancing in her direction. So predictable.

Arrogance was always Richard's Achilles' heel. It simply didn't occur to him that anyone would be watching. Jess grinned again inside the black ski mask she wore over her head and face.

Richard climbed the stairs and covered the short distance to the first door on the right while Jess watched from the shadows. He paused. The nightlights she'd placed illuminated him enough that the camera would record perfectly.

As if he followed Jess's script, Richard wore no head covering. He showed his face to avoid frightening his daughter if she awakened, to keep her quiet and not arouse her mother in the room down the hallway. Betsy's sheer terror tomorrow morning when she found Anna missing was much of what the sadist wanted to accomplish. He wanted Betsy off balance and afraid. Which she was almost all the time.

Every move Richard made reinforced Jess's sense of justification. She hadn't been near him since she was a child herself but she was satisfied that he really was the bastard she believed him to be. Reassured, she felt free to follow through without remorse.

Richard glanced around, maybe confirming that Betsy still slept soundly, that Miami PD hadn't received the silent alarm. After a moment, he opened the door to Anna's room and crept inside.

He emerged shortly with the sleeping girl in his arms. Anna was dressed in white pajamas. Strawberry curls framed her cherubic face and cascaded down the back of his arm. Partly because she always slept soundly, and partly because Jess had given her a mild sedative before bed, the child didn't stir. She hated leaving the girl in Richard's arms even a moment. Jess hoped Anna would never know anything about this evening and would sleep straight through.

Richard eased the door almost closed, leaving it as Betsy had when she saw her daughter last so that she wouldn't know Anna was gone until she saw the empty bed. *Bastard.* He descended the stairs in silence but for a stifled sneeze.

Jess waited. Her right hand held the Glock firmly pointed in Richard's direction. She'd shoot him only if he forced her to. But shoot him, she would. He'd be a fool to believe otherwise.

She *knew* Richard. If he saw her before she was ready, he would do something stupid. Something that might hurt Anna. The child's safety was paramount. Jess steadied herself and remained invisible as long as possible.

Richard snuck out the back door and closed it without a sound. Only then did she move.

Jess activated the tiny camera she wore in a pendant around her neck, waited until she heard the creaking boards under his feet and three sneezes in a row before she hurried silently out behind him. A cool breeze brushed across her eyes and lips, the only uncovered parts of her body.

She followed Richard off the property and onto the street where he'd parked a dark SUV. A less arrogant man might have noticed he was being followed. Richard did not. Now. Now he'd taken Anna in the eyes of the law. Jess wasted no time gloating.

He was bent over, placing Anna in the back seat when Jess came up behind him and pressed the Glock briefly to his spine before she widened the distance between them beyond his arm's reach.

"Move away from the car. Much as I'd like to shoot you…" She allowed her husky voice to trail away. Disuse and fear had stolen the moisture from her mouth, but she refused to acknowledge it. She moved her tongue imperceptibly seeking saliva.

Richard stepped back, cavalierly raised both hands palms out, as if he was play-acting with a child.

"Turn around," she said, quietly, hoping not to awaken Anna. He complied. He saw the gun, pointed now at his chest. He smirked.

"Smile," she said, picking up the pendant and pointing the micro camera directly toward him. "A picture's worth a year of testimony, isn't it?"

She snapped three photographs of Anna sleeping in the vehicle, too. Each image would be date and time stamped. Evidence. The more, the better.

She'd argued with Betsy and her sister, Bette, for hours about the next part of their plan. Betsy had cried, said she didn't want her child's father incarcerated. She wasn't desperate enough yet.

But Jess knew Betsy would be more desperate later; it was a mistake not to finish this now, once and for all. Richard would never give up as long as he drew free breath. Letting him go was a stupid mistake. Yet this was not her decision to make.

The breeze had picked up force and dried her eyeballs each time it brushed across, yet she refused to blink. Too much could happen in the blink of an eye. Peter was stolen in what seemed just such a quick moment fifteen years ago.

Jess held the gun steady and waited for Richard to make his move. Maybe he would give her the excuse she needed to do what should be done. Could she shoot him if she had to? *In a New York second.*

Released and alone, Richard would steal his daughter again, not because he loved her, but because he *owned* her. Anna would never be safe from him. Ever. He should have gone to prison long ago for battering his wife. Or when he stole Anna the last two times. But Betsy had refused to testify against him. Now, Jess had proof when Betsy needed it. But it would have been so much better if Betsy had agreed to Jess's final solution. Jess knew Richard was a fatal enemy, not a mere opponent.

Richard stared at Jess, wary but unafraid. He seemed to know her, but not recognize her simultaneously. His puzzlement was almost comical.

Jess's slender frame was indistinguishable from a slight man's in these clothes. And she held an equalizer pointed at his heart. Did he recognize her voice? Maybe, although they hadn't talked in years and he'd been through a lot of women since then.

She could almost see him calculating his next move and five moves after that, like a chess match. Richard had always been good at strategic games.

Jess said what she'd agreed to say. "If you ever set foot in the state of Florida again, the video of tonight's escapade will be delivered to the U.S. Attorney's office. You'll die in prison."

He smirked again. He wasn't afraid of her. He was a fool.

Jess's hand itched to smash the gun into his face at least, but she kept calm. The video would be her shield, not his sword against her, no matter how much she'd rather finish this now.

"Move to the front of the car," she said.

He sidled to the center in front of the grille, well lit by the streetlight and far enough away. Her gaze never leaving him, the gun steady, Jess bent down and lifted the little girl. Anna stirred, but didn't waken. Jess almost cried when she smelled Anna's fabric softener and baby shampoo scents.

Bastard.

When she was sure Anna was secure in her grasp, Jess distanced herself from Richard's SUV.

"Get in and drive away," she instructed, her tone harder this time, annealed with years of hatred.

Hands in his pockets, Richard shrugged, sauntered around to the driver's side and opened the front door. Instantly, the car alarm sounded. Impossibly loud repeated long blasts of the horn invaded the suburban nighttime, blasting Jess's ears.

The cacophony awakened Anna. When she saw the black-clad apparition holding her, she began to cry and kick, yelling "Let me go! Let me go!"

Jess struggled, grabbed her tightly to keep her from taking them both down to the ground, but the gun's steady aim didn't waver.

"Hush, Anna," Jess whispered close to her ear. "It's Aunt Jess. It's okay. Be quiet now."

"Aunt Jess?" the astonished child cried, tears and screams coming to a shaky, tentative halt. She pulled the ski-mask off Jess's head in one quick grab exposing her hot face to the cool morning breeze.

Richard now had one leg into the SUV, his weight shifted toward the driver's seat. He pressed the key fob to silence the blasting horn, and then flashed his sardonic smirk again. "Nice to see you again, Jess. You didn't grow up much, did you?"

She stiffened and extended the gun, her intention clear. "Don't forget what I told you, Richard. No contact. Go."

He moved his head slowly, side to side, smirk firmly affixed. "Think again, little girl. I'm taking orders from you?" He laughed, slid into the SUV, started the engine, rolled down the window, and aimed a stare of pure hatred her way.

Jess shivered imperceptibly. She'd made an open enemy of a distant one. Somehow, he would prove he controlled her, too, along with everything else in his world, no matter what the cost.

She felt hot fear coursing through her entire body and a quick flash of insight. Could he be the one who'd stolen Peter? She'd investigated and rejected the possibility long ago because Richard didn't know Peter existed. Had she been wrong?

She couldn't speak. She held the gun steady, pointed at his head.

All pretext of the gentleness he'd shown his daughter gone, he said, "You'll be sorry you screwed me, Jess. Count on it."

The SUV's powerful engine roared louder than a six-pack of Blue Angles as he sped away in the quiet darkness of the early suburban morning.

She watched his taillights recede to red pinpoints and disappear around a corner before she whispered aloud.

"I've been sorry about that for years and years."

CHAPTER TWO

THE NEWS FROM THE amber alert Internet subscription service flashed across her computer as she worked on revisions to her most recent investigative article for *Taboo Magazine*. She ignored the alert several times until she reached a logical stopping point. A domestic violence call in a Miami neighborhood. Every nerve in her body vibrated the instant Jess read the address. Eyebrows gathered at the bridge of her nose reflecting her pain when she squeezed her eyes shut and covered her face with both hands in the only brief moment of regret she allowed herself now. More pain would follow, as it should.

Her fingers shook as she worked the keys for information, hoping she was wrong while certain she wasn't.

The first officer at the scene found a woman shot and a five-year-old girl missing. An amber alert went out at 4:15 a.m. Jess glanced down at the clock on the screen. Twenty-five minutes ago. Wasting no time on useless recriminations, she left immediately.

Thirty minutes later, she reached Saturn Circle, a few houses scattered around the cul-de-sac bordering Lake Tarpon. Miami PD cruisers blocked the Dolphin Avenue entrance. Jess parked the rental and slipped her Glock under the front seat. She had a license to carry, but no need to make this tense situation worse.

She grabbed her laptop and approached the first officer she saw.

"Hey, Randy," she said, as powerfully as she could muster simply to avoid startling him in the darkness. She showed her ID. She'd been working in Miami for several weeks on another story. The cops she'd met were helpful and sympathetic. No one wanted to help crime victims within the bounds of the law more than Jess did, and she always made sure local law enforcement knew that. They were all on the same team, she felt.

Officer Randy Wilson wagged his head, rubbed his neck. "Sorry. No media inside. What's your interest, anyway?"

Jess met his steady gaze. "Betsy Martin is a crime victim. I came to offer support."

"She doesn't need it," Randy told her, too bluntly.

Jess released her breath in a long exhale, closed her eyes. The news hit her hard in the gut, even though she'd expected it, really. Pressing a man like Richard as hard as she'd done was dangerous. She'd known it at the time, but she'd thought the stakes were worth it. A short moment of guilty mourning was all she permitted herself for now. Plenty of time for remorse later, too.

"Suspects?"

"Nasty divorce. Custody problems with the daughter."

Jess nodded to draw him out, not trusting her voice to remain steady just yet.

"Bet on the ex," Randy said. His tone conveyed the disgust only the well-informed would feel. "Real piece of shit. Restraining orders, my ass."

Nobody needed to tell her how inadequate the law was at protecting women from men like Richard.

"Can I go up?" *While my legs will still carry me?*

He shrugged again, nodded, as if to suggest there was no harm she could do at this point. "Why not?"

"Who's primary?" she asked.

"Jerry Schmidt. Missing persons."

Jess shivered in the morning's cool breeze, wishing she'd pulled her sweater from the back seat. She made her way down the short street to the brick colonial at the end. She saw two unmarked cars, an ambulance, and people milling around. Officers, crime scene technicians, photographers.

A couple of detectives interviewing a woman, maybe one of the neighbors, maybe the one who'd called in the gunshots. Tallish woman, mid-forties probably. Hair gathered at her nape. Very pregnant. She made a mental note to interview the woman later, if she needed to.

Jess walked up the sidewalk to the threshold and stared into the open front door.

Betsy Martin's body lay on the tiled foyer floor, clad in a neon yellow nightgown, eyes open, frozen in surprise. Two entrance wounds were visible in her chest and abdomen. Lots of blood had pooled. Bullets probably severed the femoral artery. No way Betsy would have survived, even if she'd been found immediately. The thought was little comfort. Betsy's body had been there a while, long enough for all the blood to have congealed. Jess closed her eyes briefly and offered a silent prayer. For Betsy, Anna, and herself.

She moved carefully through the foyer. A few feet inside, Jess caught Detective Schmidt's attention.

"I heard you were in town again," he said, a question in his tone that she'd answered too many times before. *Why?* That's what he wanted to know.

"Betsy Martin was a friend. I thought maybe I could help you find Anna," she said. She might have told him the whole story if Betsy was still alive. Now, that's all he needed to know.

He sized her up as if he'd never seen her before, although the two had worked together on a case last year. He might have sent her packing except time was of the essence and an abducted child was their number one priority. He waved toward the body. "Not a pretty scene."

Jess glanced briefly at Betsy, but she'd already seen more than she wanted to.

"There are security cameras throughout the house and grounds." She pointed to the camera hidden in the wall sconce on the side of the front door. When his eyebrows rose in question, she nodded to convey a certainty she couldn't voice. "They might help."

Schmidt seemed to consider something, but after a few moments he said, "We're not through processing yet. Don't touch anything else." He let her pass.

Jess focused on the work. She moved carefully through the kitchen, Anna's room, Betsy's room, and the door that led outside to the attached garage. She located the surveillance cameras she'd insisted Betsy install and removed the memory cards. The cameras recorded in a loop, replacing images every three days. Maybe they'd get lucky.

One of the techs gave her permission to set up on the kitchen table where she'd waited for Richard Martin on that dark night last year. The bright kitchen lights blazed now, bathing modern steel appliances and glossy surfaces that reflected harshly. Uniformed personnel from multiple agencies moved about as if choreographed by Broadway. No mingling, no collisions, but rising noise levels as equipment was moved in and out, evidence was collected, and the crime scene was both secured and processed. No time wasted, either.

Jess opened her laptop, booted up, and slipped the memory card from the kitchen camera into the slot first. The images downloaded quickly. She and Detective Schmidt watched video of the dark kitchen, but nothing more.

"It was a long shot," he said, by way of forgiveness.

Methodically, Jess downloaded data from the other four and continued searching. "Look there." She pointed to the screen. The intruder had come in through the garage door.

"Who is it?" Scanlon asked, as if he truly couldn't guess. A test, perhaps.

"Richard Martin." No surprise and no doubt about it, either. *He's a bold bastard*, she reminded herself. She swiped a palm across her eyes.

Together, they studied the digital images on the laptop screen. She felt a sick *déjà vu* as she watched Richard invade the house, disarm the security system, climb the stairs, enter Anna's room and return carrying the sleeping girl, as he'd done the night Jess had watched him from this very kitchen chair.

"Dammit!" she muttered. She should have forced Betsy to turn Richard in last year. If she had, Betsy would be alive now; Anna wouldn't be missing.

"Look," Schmidt pointed to the image.

She shook off her scolding and watched Richard reach the bottom of the stairs, his body twisted to the right, toward the garage door this time instead of the back patio.

Almost instantly, bright light flooded the foyer with the flip of a single switch at the base of the stairs.

Camera three had captured the entire scene.

Eerily, Betsy stood alive very near the same location she was laying dead now. "Richard!" her voice screeched like an outraged Valkyrie even from the laptop's inadequate speakers. Jess winced.

Anna awakened, looked around, sleepy-eyed, disoriented.

"Daddy?" she said, as if she was surprised to be held in his arms. Which surely she was. He hadn't seen her in fourteen months, and the last time was under harrowing circumstances.

"Put her down, Richard! Don't you dare take her out that door!" Betsy's panicked screech instructed.

"Okay." He chuckled, changed direction and strode past her, toward the front door instead.

Betsy grabbed his arm, jerking it from under Anna's legs.

Richard grasped the child tighter, held her close to his chest. Then, in a quick jerk, he yanked his right arm from Betsy's grasp, reached around his back, slipped a .38 from his belt, and shot her twice. The entire maneuver swiftly executed, as if he'd practiced it until muscle memory supplied all needed direction.

Betsy fell to the floor like a crumpled doll.

Anna screamed, "Mommy! Mommy!" and began to thrash wildly.

Richard held onto the frightened girl despite her screaming, thrashing panic. He strode through the front door and out of camera range. Anna's screams faded as he moved further away from the house.

The screen next reflected the empty foyer captured by the fixed lens of camera three. The scene was grisly enough; the authentic sounds were overwhelmingly heartbreaking. Jess could hardly bear to hear it, but neither could she show her feelings to these men or turn away. Betsy endured the pain; Jess served merely to witness.

After an excruciating lifetime of seconds, Betsy's ever-fainter groans simply stopped.

Moments of stunned silence followed from the gathered professionals.

Schmidt laid a hand on Jess's shoulder, perhaps as small comfort. "We'll get a warrant and an APB. Any idea where he's taken the girl?"

Numb, she said, "He's a Canadian citizen. Lives in Toronto. Wealthy."

Schmidt sighed, resignation showing in the slump of his shoulders. "If he gets her to Canada before we catch him, that's a big problem."

"Why?"

"Canada won't extradite him for a crime that carries the death penalty. And we won't waive the death penalty unless he pleads guilty and accepts a life sentence."

Jess's despair suddenly overwhelmed her. She blinked back tears. "I can see that happening all right."

Schmidt nodded. "Sarcasm won't help. There are some alternatives. None are perfect and they all take time."

"You'll understand if I don't think spending the next two years cutting through bureaucratic red tape to get Anna back through channels is a great solution." Her voice broke. She took a few deep breaths to steady herself. Falling apart wouldn't help Betsy. Or Anna. Or Peter. Jess tried desperately not to think about Peter.

She cued up the last of the video again and checked the time stamp on the image. "He's been gone more than six hours. By private plane, he could easily be in Toronto already."

"Private plane?" Schmidt asked.

Jess nodded. Richard wouldn't have risked a commercial flight.

"We'll check the airlines to be sure," Schmidt paused, ran a hand over his bald head. "Otherwise, I'm afraid we're done here, Jess. He's gone six hours. We won't find him inside this country."

"But you're going to try."

"We'll try." He blew a long, frustrated stream of air out of his nostrils. "Of course, we'll try. Is the girl an American citizen?"

"What the hell does that matter?" If Jess sounded like she was spoiling for a fight, it's because she was. The idea of beating Richard to a bloody pulp sounded perfectly delightful at the moment. If he'd been standing in the room, she might have tried it. Most of the others present would have piled on, she was sure.

"We've got a lot of unsolved cases on the books, Jess. More coming in every day. We can't spend our resources tilting at windmills. We'll turn it over to the Feds if we can't do anything else." He paused.

"But?"

Gently, Schmidt said, "But we have to face reality. For Miami PD, this case is probably closed."

Jess felt a slow burn rising from her toes to the top of her hair. Every nerve ending alert. Betsy dead. Anna missing. Richard Martin gone.

Case closed?

Not a chance.

CHAPTER THREE

AFTER THE FIFTH LAP, cold rain pelting her body, punishing her for screwing up, Jess began to feel a bit better. Although her college racing days were long over, running still cleared her head. The rain slid over her wet skin. She completed a turn around the track and kept pounding, one foot and then the other. She used the steady rhythm that allowed her mind to strategize. The problem wasn't finding Richard. Despite what Schmidt had said, locating Richard would be fairly simple. Jess knew where to look. She'd been watching him for years.

Extracting Anna from Canada was another matter entirely. A much knottier problem. Every solution she tested got pounded to bits by her feet on the cinders.

And if she managed it, somehow, then keeping the girl away from Richard in the future seemed impossible. Hadn't Betsy tried to do precisely that and ended up dead?

Jess had briefly considered becoming a lawyer, years ago, after college. But the authorities searching for Peter, and their failure to find him, left her disillusioned and angry with the law's all-consuming workload as well as its compromises and failures.

The system focused on the rights of criminals, in Jess's view, when it should be more concerned with crime's victims.

All these years later, she was glad she'd chosen investigative journalism instead. She'd quickly discovered she loved the work. It satisfied her in a way she'd never expected while she searched for Peter. And it allowed her to work privately for crime victims' rights when she wanted to, unencumbered by the rules lawyers and law enforcement teams were required to follow.

The lifestyle suited her, too. She traveled to research her stories, but she carefully selected worthy subjects and fashioned solutions for victims that protected them as much as possible. People like Betsy Martin and her sister, Bette. The work funded her search for Peter and fueled her resolve. She'd made the right choices, after a rocky start. Every day she prayed she'd turned her life around before it was too late for Peter. But had she?

Jess frowned and shook rainwater from her eyes and Peter from her thinking. *Focus.* Richard would never leave *his* child alone unless he was in prison or dead. There was no middle ground for Anna. Jess must resolve that problem, too. She needed a permanent solution.

Jess ran, one foot and then the other, pounding the cinders, lap after lap, ignoring the wind and rain that chilled her. Her plan resolved, she finished by walking twice around, allowing the icy rain to drench her body. The cool air now felt refreshing because she knew what she was going to do. Maybe her plan wouldn't work. Maybe she'd end up like Betsy. Maybe Richard would win once more. But she had to try. For Peter. She dropped her gaze to the ground and headed into the showers.

CHAPTER FOUR

JESS WAITED LONG ENOUGH for Richard to relax into complacency and Anna to regain some composure before she flew from Miami to Buffalo. At the airport she rented an anonymous-looking gray sedan. She'd rejected a non-stop flight to Toronto. Although faster and easier, she'd be dependent on flight schedules for the return. Since 9/11, airport security had become irritatingly problematic. She'd be required to prove Anna's identity, which would make them easier to stop and trace. No, driving into and out of Canada was best.

Reluctantly, she rejected buying an untraceable gun on the streets of Buffalo. Taking a gun into Canada was a serious crime. Canadian citizens weren't allowed to carry concealed weapons. Even owning them was severely restricted. If she was caught she'd be arrested and probably imprisoned. Anna would certainly be returned to her father. No, the risk was too great. She'd take Anna away from Richard permanently using guile alone. She refused to fail again.

Jess drove to Lewiston, New York, and checked into a mom-and-pop motel. She rented the room for two nights. Tomorrow, she'd test her plan. The following day, she'd execute it.

She slept lightly for four hours, then dressed casually in khaki slacks, pink shirt, blue blazer, and running shoes. She fluffed her curly blonde hair and studied herself in the mirror, pleased by the guileless soccer mom effect she'd created.

It was dark at five a.m. as she drove toward the Lewiston-Queenston Bridge. If he thought about her at all, Richard would expect her to take the shortest route to and from Toronto. She intended to oblige. Drive time was seventy-five minutes, barring construction or heavy traffic.

The border crossing went well. Off season, during the week, the area was almost deserted both ways. Very few travelers meant only one of the two customs booths was open. As in most of the small tourist towns, the Canadian customs officer simply asked her name, nationality, where she was going and when she planned to return. She'd offered the typical tourist's response for a visit to Niagara Falls and paid the toll. He'd waved her through without asking for ID. *May the return be so easy,* she thought, wiping the sweat from each palm onto her slacks.

She reached the private school where her research revealed Anna was enrolled. After circling the block twice to be sure Richard wasn't lurking and didn't have Anna under surveillance, she parked in front. She had a clear view of the playground while waiting for 10:15 a.m. It nagged her that Richard seemed to have allowed Anna out of his control. Was he that sure of himself? Had he arrogantly assumed Jess had given up? If so, he didn't know her at all. That thought comforted more than the alternatives.

At 10:20, a young woman led twenty energetic children out the door to the playground. Jess spotted Anna. When she saw the little girl with the strawberry curls for the first time, Jess's eyes teared. She wiped her eyes with her fingers, willing the tears away. No time for sorrow now. She pushed all emotion aside as luxury. The job demanded her full attention.

Anna seemed quiet and unfocused, but functional. Eyes dull and heavy-lidded, she stood apart from the other children clutching a rag doll under her left arm and sucking her right thumb.

A low flame of denied anger began in Jess's stomach. Anna's parents had been locked into their own rage, unable to put Anna's life first. The child would never be normal again. Anna was a victim of a tragic struggle. All Jess could do now was try to mitigate the damage. And get the bastard responsible. And maybe, someday, make it up to her by uniting her with her brother.

Richard Martin was no kind of father. Never to Peter, and not to Anna, either. The knowledge soothed Jess's guilt only slightly.

Like every good investigator, she'd analyzed the risks, then constructed Plan A and Plan B. Plan A: she and Anna returned home without Richard's interference, luring him back into the U.S. where authorities would arrest him. Plan B provided an alternative if Richard attempted to thwart her. He would be dealt with at the border crossing. At least, in theory.

Yet again, she regretted the decision she'd had to make about the gun and prayed her alternative would work, even though it could cost Jess her own life. She'd no alternatives left.

CHAPTER FIVE

AS ALWAYS BEFORE EXECUTING the final stages of any plan, Jess slept fitfully. Finally, at 4:00 a.m., she gave up the effort. She dressed again in yesterday's costume and launched Plan A.

Jess arrived at the school two hours early and parked down the street, waiting for Anna's arrival. Just before nine, a station wagon stopped. A young woman helped Anna out of the back seat, and held her hand as they walked to the school's front entrance. The woman was gentle with Anna, but Anna demonstrated no affection when they parted. Anna walked into the school, slowly and alone, dragging the rag doll with her. The woman returned to the station wagon and left.

Jess felt anger's slow burn ignite in her gut. Teeth clenched, muscles tense. She willed her breathing and heartbeat's slowing, even pace. Anger now would only interfere with her performance. Another luxury for later.

When the children entered the playground for recess, Jess left her car and strolled over. She called to Anna twice. The child looked up. A broad grin slowly lit her face. Anna loped toward her.

"Aunt Jess!" she said, crying as Jess picked her up and hugged her, too tightly. She felt thinner inside her clothes. Jess's sadness, followed by hot anger, returned and she allowed herself to feel, just briefly.

Within a few moments, Jess had explained to Anna's teacher that Anna had a dentist's appointment and produced a forged note from Richard allowing her to take the child. The teacher looked at Jess carefully, but released Anna, probably in part because Anna continued to hold onto Jess as if she never wanted to let go. Less than fifteen minutes after Jess first saw Anna on the playground, they were driving toward Lewiston. So far, Plan A seemed to be working.

Constantly checking the rearview mirror, she retraced the route she'd taken the day before. Anna, securely belted in the back seat, had returned to her subdued behavior. She talked quietly to the rag doll she'd brought along with her. About an hour into the drive, her eyelids closed, her chin gently touched her chest and she fell into the rhythm of sleep. A bit of drool slid from the corner of her mouth onto the doll's head. She was so young, so sweet. So undeserving of this mess. Jess clenched the steering wheel so tight her hands cramped.

Was Richard controlling Anna with medication of some kind? Another thing to despise him for. Jess glanced at her watch. Just like yesterday, she was right on time. Even the weather cooperated.

When they approached the border crossing, Jess located the passports, prepared to show them if she had to. She'd seen no sign of Richard or anyone following her for the entire return trip, which worried her.

Richard was crazy, violent, controlling. She'd expected him to know where Anna was every second, and to come after her. Or at least, Richard should have learned Anna was abducted and reasoned that Jess would take the shortest route back to the U.S.

So far, she hadn't seen Richard. But her senses were on alert. She'd finally learned never to underestimate him. There was something she'd missed. Somehow, she believed, when they reached the border, he'd be there. Then what? She'd already decided. Plan B. Could she pull it off?

Supremely focused now, she drove over the bridge without noticing the spectacular views of Niagara Gorge. At the U.S. check point, the line of vehicles moved swiftly through a single open kiosk. She looked into the cinder-block customs building, which also housed the duty free store. She saw one officer behind the counter, and one clerk in the store waiting on a customer.

While she watched, the customer carried a bottle of liquor in a plain brown bag to the rusty battered panel van waiting in line in front of Jess's vehicle and got in. The panel van belched smoke when it backfired, and its muffler had long ago surrendered to the rust belt.

Mid-week, off season, at lunch time, the entire area was relaxed, thinly patrolled and almost deserted. She hoped this would make Richard more obvious, if he appeared and tried anything.

Jess mentally rehearsed the lie she'd tell if the customs officer asked her more than routine questions. Yesterday, the process was casual, easy, intended to encourage tourism, not to thwart a kidnapper. Would it be the same today? *Please, God.*

Two cars ahead passed through the checkpoint. Only one more ahead of her. When the panel van jerked toward the kiosk window, Jess pulled up and waited at the yellow line. The van blocked her view of the officer.

She glanced around the entire vicinity and saw nothing unusual. Then, looked again toward the duty-free store. She saw a lone figure, vaguely familiar, standing outside.

Could it be?

Richard.

He'd shaved his head and wore sunglasses. But it was him. Definitely. He couldn't disguise his arrogance.

She didn't know how he'd found her, but he had and she wasn't surprised. She'd expected him, knew he'd come. But how?

A tracking device on Anna somewhere? Regular calls to the school just to check on his daughter?

However he'd managed it, he was here now. She had to move. Adrenaline made her heart pound and sweat bead on her brow. No choice now. Plan B.

Stay calm.

Checking the rearview, she realized she'd have to move forward. An eighteen-wheeler six feet behind blocked any alternative, even if she'd wanted to leave the line and return deeper into Canada. Which she didn't. What she needed to do was leave the country. Now.

The officer in the kiosk seemed to be chatting too long with the occupants of the panel van. But she couldn't see the officer and he couldn't see her. She tapped the steering wheel impatiently with her thumbs.

Mimicking the guy who'd joined the van earlier, Richard strolled toward her car. Quiet panic fluttered in her chest as she watched him. Did anyone else see? He reached her car door, looked directly into her eyes as if to mesmerize her, grasped the handle, and lifted it.

The locked door didn't open. He glanced then into the back seat where Anna slept, covered by the blanket Jess had brought, still holding the doll. The normal sarcastic smirk creased his face. Insight struck.

It was the doll. That's where he'd hidden the tracking device.

Bastard. You think you're so clever. We'll see.

Jess lowered the back window and Richard stuck his left hand on the top of the glass, gripped as if he might pull the glass out. His right hand gripped the passenger door handle.

"Go away, Richard, while you still can. If you try anything here, border patrol will kill you. Your choice."

He laughed. "I'm touched that you'd care. Truly. But you're kidnapping my daughter, Jess. Do you really think they'll take your side over mine?"

While he held onto the glass and the door handle Jess punched the accelerator. The car leaped forward. Richard lost his balance. She slammed the brake. The car's quick jerk threw him to the ground. Her actions, and Richard's, were blocked from the customs officer's view by the panel van, which moved forward now, slowly, through the open gate.

Maybe surveillance cameras saw him. Surely, the border guards would protect her and the child. She hoped.

The officer inside the booth waved her ahead. She released a breath and eased to stop next to the booth, left hand on the wheel.

"What's your citizenship, ma'am?" the kindly old officer asked.

"U.S." She glanced in the right side mirror. Richard had risen from the ground. His stare carried a malevolence she could feel. *Bastard. Go away. While you still can.*

The customs officer glanced into the back seat now, too,

where Anna slept. At the same time, he noticed Richard, hands in the oversized pocket of his sweatshirt, standing too close, not moving, saying nothing.

The officer became more alert. "How about the child, ma'am?" Another officer came out of the building, hand on his gun, waiting.

They *had* seen Richard try to enter her car. It was working. Plan B was working. *Thank God.*

"U.S., too." Small rivulets of sweat tickled her armpits. *Let us go, Richard, and live to try again.*

"Picture I.D., Ma'am?"

Jess reached into her handbag, retrieved the passports and handed them to the officer. He examined the blue jacketed folders. "Your name is Jessica Kimball? And hers is Anna Martin?"

"Divorce," she said. Richard simply stood there. What was he thinking? Was he willing to die to thwart her?

The big truck behind her seemed to breathe fire through its roaring engine when the driver tapped his accelerator impatiently. Jess felt the heat rolling toward her.

The officer glanced at Richard again. Maybe experience, or training or something gave him an uneasy pang. Now, his full attention was focused on the situation. "Do you have the child's birth certificate?"

Jess furrowed her brow with mock consternation. "I didn't think you'd need it."

He closed the passports and gestured toward the building. "I'm sorry, Ma'am. Park over there and go inside where they'll verify your identification." Then he nodded at Richard, who stood stock-still, feet braced shoulder width apart, hands still inside his big front pocket. "Do you know him?"

Now. Plan B. Now was the time. *Do it!*

She took a breath. Exhaled. "He's got a gun."

Before the officer could react, Richard slowly extracted his hand from the sweatshirt, and pointed the gun at her head.

"Get down! Get down!" the officer shouted, squatting beside the car's engine block, the only place safe from gunfire.

In that instant, Richard chose death.

The deafening noise of shots rang out. Bullets entered the rear glass. One grazed Jess's arm as she fell sideways. Another exited inches from where her head had been an instant before. The pain seared through her as blood soaked her blazer and ran down her arm. Anna began to scream.

Border guards acted immediately. They shouted for Richard to drop his gun. He didn't.

A guard shot and hit Richard in the leg. He went down, and kept shooting.

Bullets tattooed the back of the sedan. Anna's screams intensified.

Idiot! You'll hit Anna!

After an excruciatingly long few moments, the customs officer in the booth drew his weapon, and two additional officers ran out from the building. "Drop your gun! Drop your gun!"

Jess looked into Richard's eyes. Either of them could have changed things at that moment.

But they didn't.

Plan B. She jammed the accelerator to the floorboard. The sedan lurched forward, broke through the wooden gate, and raced onto American soil.

Richard shot at Jess's car again. As she'd known they would, the guards returned fire.

Jess mashed the brake, jerking the sedan to a stop behind the solid walls of the U.S. Customs station. Applying pressure to her throbbing, bleeding arm, she managed to open the back door and unsnap Anna's seatbelt. She slid the hysterical child onto the pavement and held Anna close, shielding her, until the deafening gunfire stopped.

In the brief silence, Anna's screams became wailing sobs. Jess struggled to rise while holding the girl despite the searing pain in her arm, and stumbled back to view the scene at the kiosk. Richard lay on the ground, blood running from his mouth, lifeless eyes staring straight at her. Her first thought was, *Thank God.*

Jess's anger flared. He'd chosen to die rather than let Jess take Anna. He'd intended to get all three of them killed. Instead, Peter's father breathed life no more.

At that moment, Jess felt no remorse. Maybe she would be sorry some day, when Peter asked, "Why did you let them kill my father?" But not now.

CHAPTER SIX

A FEW DAYS LATER, Jess joined Bette, who sat watching Anna on the Land of the Dragons playground. The family resemblance was unmistakable. Both were clearly from Betsy Martin's gene pool. In Anna, Jess saw some hint of Richard too. How could a wonderful child have emerged from two such damaged parents?

The woman Jess had seen outside Betsy's house the night of the shooting was there, too. Maria Gaspar's youngest daughter and Anna were friends. Both girls were on the playground.

"She looks happy, doesn't she?" Bette asked, with a wistful tone. Anna was in counseling and taking medication which the psychologist hoped would help her to work through the traumas she'd endured at her parents' hands.

To reassure her, Jess said, "Don't worry so much. She's young. With luck and love, she won't remember most of it."

A tear rolled down Bette's cheek. Her lips quivered. "She won't have much to remember about her mother."

Jess closed her eyes against tears of her own. She had risked her life so that Anna might thrive. Now, all she could do was hope. "It's up to you to keep Betsy alive for her."

"We'll help, too, Bette," Maria said, giving Bette's shoulders a hug and meeting Jess's gaze over Bette's bowed head. "Carlos has been like a father to Anna for a while now, anyway."

Jess nodded her agreement to this imperfect arrangement. Together, they watched Anna climb the rope ladders and slide down the dragon's tail, laughing when she landed on her butt in the sand.

"Betsy was so smitten. And he loved her, too." Bette stopped, bewildered. "What went wrong?"

Jess rubbed her sore arm to stop its pulsing. Like Richard's effect on Anna, Jess's wound would hurt for a long time and leave a permanent scar. Jess needed no reminder of the hole in her heart where Peter lived, but welcomed the pain and would welcome the scar, too. She'd narrowly escaped Richard twice. She never intended to forget that, or to make the same mistake again.

She rejected sweetening the truth. To defeat Richard forever, Bette must do her part. "Betsy knew he was dangerous before she married him. She ignored her instincts and deceived herself. I'll help you, but the best thing you can do for Betsy now is to make sure Anna doesn't repeat that pattern."

And I'll be watching.

THE END

FATAL
EDGE

CAST OF CHARACTERS

Jessica Kimball
Mandy Donovan
Trent Brennan
Carl Asher
Jim Kubiak

CHAPTER ONE

TRENT TUGGED HIS COAT more tightly around him as he walked through the bitter cold toward the building that housed *Taboo Magazine's* offices in downtown Denver. He kept his head down and made his way along the sidewalk through the frigid winter wind. On the way, he planned his approach.

Mandy Donovan had a journalism degree, and she worked for *Taboo's* Jess Kimball as the relentless reporter's assistant, but she wanted to stretch her skills. If he could talk Mandy into going away with him for the weekend, they could combine business with pleasure.

Trent was smitten with Mandy the first time he saw her. But now, after a few weeks of dating, he felt like the luckiest man alive. Not only was Mandy gorgeous, she also had a straightforward personality that Trent found refreshingly delightful. He was plain-spoken himself, so he appreciated the trait in others.

He hoped Mandy felt the same way about him. She'd definitely be an asset on this new case he'd just picked up. By the time he reached the building and shoved the door open, his eyes were stinging from the cold, and he almost missed the cell phone vibrating in his pocket.

"Trent Brennan Investigations," he said without looking at the caller ID. He stamped the snow from his boots on the mat.

"You took the case yesterday, and I've heard nothing from you yet. For the fee we're paying you, Brennan, we expect fast results," Francine Lloyd sniffed into the phone with ever-present disdain. "I'll require constant updates, so make sure you keep your phone handy."

The call was disconnected before he even had a chance to reply and Trent shot his phone a glare and tucked it back into his pocket. "Sure thing, your highness," he mumbled under his breath.

He gave himself a quick attitude adjustment. This was a potentially lucrative job. It certainly promised to pay more than anything else he'd taken on since he opened his own firm. The kind of publicity and referrals the Lloyds could give him if the case went well simply couldn't be bought.

But neither could he. If Mrs. Lloyd thought pressuring him would get her an unethical supply of false evidence to support her son's innocence, she'd find herself sadly disappointed. Integrity was the only thing he had to sell, and he'd never get his new business off the ground if he abandoned his own rules.

He stepped away from the bitter cold drafting through the revolving door and deeper into the warm lobby, making his way to the elevators. *Taboo's* offices were near the top of the building. He left the elevator and grinned when he caught sight of Mandy. She was hunkered down at a small conference room table with her hands wrapped around a giant steaming mug. Coffee, probably. She drank it hot, black, and all day long.

"Please tell me you have more coffee," he murmured,

folding his gloved hands together in mock prayer.

Mandy's face went pink with pleasure, and she stood, pressing a warm kiss to his icy cheek. "I didn't expect you until lunch time. Come with me."

He followed her to the coffee station where he filled a large paper cup with plenty of java juice and tried to stop shivering.

"I'm so sorry to interrupt." He flashed an apologetic smile.

She shook her head and waved him off. "I just finished up a phone call with Jess. She's out on a story."

"Isn't she always? Jess Kimball has got to be the hardest working reporter in the magazine biz." The coffee was doing its job, and he warmed up enough to unbutton his coat.

"Does she have a new lead on her missing boy?" He liked Jess a lot. He appreciated her no-nonsense attitude and the way she took on the justice system every day. Not to mention her unwavering commitment to finding her missing son. Growing up as a latch-key kid with a mother who had done the bare minimum and then kicked him out at age eighteen, Trent couldn't help but admire the hell out of Jess Kimball.

A cloud settled over Mandy's pretty face as she shook her head. "Not that I know of. She has a whole team of investigators searching every new lead that comes up. But after all these years…"

"If she needs another P.I. on the team, I'm ready, willing, and able." His teeth had stopped chattering, finally.

"I'll let her know." Mandy led the way to the conference room, and Trent followed.

He said, "I was hoping to get her take on my new case, though. Will Jess be back in town soon?"

"She'll be happy to help if she can, I'm sure." Mandy loved working on cases with Jess. Her job was to do a lot of the digging Jess needed, and she was good at it. "What kind of case is it?"

"Missing person at this point, but they're not sure whether it was a kidnapping, a runaway, or a murder." Trent tossed his coat on a chair and sat across from her.

Mandy's eyes went sharp as she scanned Trent's face for answers. "A missing child?"

"No, no." He shook his head quickly. "A young woman. She and her fiancé were at a ski lodge in Black Pines, Wyoming, about a month ago. He says they went to bed that night and when he woke up, she was gone and their room door was ajar. She hasn't been seen since." He paused to take a sip of the piping hot brew and groaned. "Thanks, I needed that."

Mandy gave him a distracted smile. "No problem. Did her family hire you to try to find her or…?"

This was where things might get a little tricky.

"Actually, no. I got a call from DeRamo, Stein, and Fletcher."

"The big blue chip law firm on 17th Street?" Mandy asked, her tone almost as chilly as Trent's cheeks.

"That's the one," he replied lightly. "They represent the fiancé, Alex Lloyd."

Mandy's eyes widened. "Alex Lloyd, Jr.? Heir to the Lloyd's Oil & Gas fortune?"

"The one and only." Trent nodded and sipped the coffee again. "He's being squeezed hard, both by the cops and the woman's family. The Lloyds feel like enough is enough. Their business is suffering from the negative publicity, and they want an independent investigator to go out to shake loose the truth. Maybe come up with an alternative theory to the one the cops are clinging to."

"Which is?" Mandy frowned.

"That Alex Lloyd murdered his fiancé Rebecca after they had a fight because she caught him cheating, and then hid the body somewhere out in the wilderness." He paused. "There's been so much terrible weather there that dogs have been no help."

"It's been a nasty winter everywhere, it seems. We've had more than our share of snow and record low temps here in Denver, too." Mandy's frown deepened, and she folded her hands on the table.

"Right. Well, Rebecca's family wants answers long before the spring thaw." Trent took a deep breath and plunged ahead. "Needless to say, they've been pushing local law enforcement, making sure they're working the case night and day. Between the family and the cops, somebody's on top of Alex Lloyd twenty-four-seven."

"As they should be, if he's guilty," Mandy muttered.

This was what he'd feared. Jess Kimball's whole career had been built on supporting victim's rights. She didn't give a rat's ass about the Alex Lloyds of the world if they were guilty. Stood to reason that Mandy would feel the same way.

"Do you think she's dead? And do you think he killed her?" Mandy asked. "Because if he killed her, Jess wouldn't get involved in helping him prove otherwise. *Taboo* wouldn't cover a case like that, either. It's pure sensationalism."

Trent shrugged. "Can't rule either of those things out. But just because he and his parents are entitled snobs doesn't mean he's a murderer. I need to approach it with an open mind. He's entitled to the presumption of innocence, just like anybody else."

He didn't add that the Lloyds offered to double his fee for "positive results." That piece of information was irrelevant. His personal financial crisis didn't mean Alex Lloyd was a murderer, either.

"So why are you telling *Taboo* about this particular case?" Mandy never wasted time getting to the crux of things.

"Well, I was hoping to get Jess involved. But since she's not here, any chance you could come with me for the week?"

"To a ski lodge in Wyoming?" Mandy's big smile was a mega-watt wonder. He felt better about asking for the favor almost immediately.

"Well, yes. I could really use a second set of ears and someone to help me with research and notes and whatnot. But also…" he trailed off and offered a comically lecherous gaze. "I thought we could spend a couple of extra days out there. Like a working vacation."

"Yes. Absolutely. I'm in." Her face was alight with excitement. "But I'll need to clear it with Jess."

"I'd love to have her come with us. She could bring a date, too. My client's paying."

"Because they think Jess would feature the story in *Taboo*?" Mandy frowned again and he started to worry about permanent lines in her face.

"Of course not, no one can promise that. But if she *wanted* to do it, I doubt the Lloyds' would object."

"I'll ask her. She doesn't usually take much time off, but if there's work involved, she'd consider it, maybe." Mandy cocked her head as if she was thinking up an approach that her boss would not refuse. "When do we need to leave?"

"Thursday. And I'll have you back by the following Wednesday if that works for you?"

"Just sit there and let me call her." Mandy pushed a speed dial button and held the phone to her ear while she waited. When

Jess answered, Mandy explained the situation. After that, she put the phone on the table and pushed the speaker phone button.

"Trent, I gather the family is paying you a hefty sum for this. Does that include our expenses if we go?" The call was so clear that Jess might have been sitting in the room.

"Absolutely. I've been told that money is no concern. They just want the man cleared and the case closed."

"They realize that we could be putting the final evidence against him into the hands of the police, I assume?" Jess said.

Trent squirmed. He'd explained that to the Lloyds, but he wasn't sure they understood they'd signed up for the result, which could go either way. "I've advised them of all the potential consequences, yes. But I won't tell you they're going to like it if things turn out badly."

Silence on the open line lasted so long that Trent began to worry she'd hung up. Finally, Jess said, "I've got to finish up what I'm working on now. Mandy can get started without me. We're used to working long distance. Mandy, send me all the information Trent has collected and then you two go ahead. I'll get up to speed and join you in Wyoming if you still need me by the time I'm finished here. How's that?"

Trent gave Mandy a grudging smile and pushed his chair back from the table. "Sounds like a plan."

"Mandy, you know you can always call me if you need me," Jess continued. "And if you get out there and things smell fishy, or they start pressuring you, just remember, you can't put a price on our integrity. Stay in touch."

"You know I will, Jess," Mandy said before she ended the call.

"Does that mean I'm on her list now, you think?" Trent asked Mandy in a low voice.

Because of her relationship with Mandy, he'd spent the past few months trying his best to make a good impression on Jess. Now he wondered if he should've kept the details to himself and simply asked Mandy to request a week of vacation.

"Believe me, if you were on her list, you'd know it. Your coffee would be frozen solid, it would be so cold in here." Mandy chuckled. "She's right at the end of another project, and things are always tense at that point. She just needs a little while to let the situation settle in, is all. As for me, I'm really glad you invited me along."

A trip together was a big step. One he hadn't intended to take for another few months, but when this job fell into his lap, it seemed like a sign. Mandy had spent the night at his house a bunch of times and things were good between them. Time to see if they could take their relationship to the next level.

If they could solve this missing person case favorably for his client while they were at it, even better.

CHAPTER TWO

"ARE YOU ALL RIGHT?" Trent eyed Mandy as she hugged her winter coat tighter around her Thursday afternoon. She adjusted her scarf for the fourth time since they'd collected the luggage and stood to wait for the shuttle from the lodge.

Not that he could blame her. He was thinking about building a fire right then and there.

Denver had been cold when they'd left, but Wyoming was downright frigid. The air was crisp and dry, punctuated by the kind of freeze that settled in the bones and made your lungs sting with every breath. Based on the dim, gray hue of the clouds, the weather would get a whole lot worse before it got better.

"Oh good, the shuttle is here!" Mandy rubbed her gloved hands together and then dragged her suitcase across the snowy ground until she reached the back of a dark blue Jeep. Trent followed, hoping to grab her bag and haul it into the trunk for her, but the shuttle driver did the job.

Mandy folded her long legs into the back seat and settled in. After depositing his gear, Trent joined her just as the wind screamed and a fresh wave of snow blew off the drift-laden trees surrounding the airport parking lot.

"Welcome. Looks like we made good time." The driver was a sweet-faced kid who looked too young for a driver's license. He pulled out into minimal traffic, tires crunching on the snow-covered road. "I'm Kyle."

"Yeah, we only just got in. We weren't waiting long." Mandy brushed snow from her hair and her jacket.

"I meant because we'll beat the weather." He shifted gears and started up the mountain road. "Weatherman says it'll be a rough one tonight. Again. We haven't had a winter this bad since I was a kid." Kyle shook his head, and Trent fought the urge to laugh. Kyle couldn't be more than eighteen years old. To Trent, he was *still* a kid.

"We're lucky, then." Mandy nodded. "I didn't realize."

"Oh yeah, when the sky gets dark this early in the day, that's how you know. Plus, of course, you can smell it." He gave them another sage nod as the jeep lurched up the mountainside. "So what brings you to Black Pines?"

Before Mandy could answer, Trent said, "I'm here to see if I can find out what happened to Rebecca Anderson. And, since the lodge is the last place she was seen alive, it seemed prudent to start there."

He hadn't planned on coming out of the gate at a canter, but the local gossip mill in this hamlet had to be running as efficiently as a fine-tuned engine. It would only be a day or two at best before everyone knew why he and Mandy were here anyway. Better to be honest from the get-go and build a little trust.

"Yeah, man. That was really sad. She seemed nice," Kyle murmured, shifting uncomfortably in his seat.

"And what about him?" Trent asked. "Alex? Was he nice too?"

"Not exactly. He wasn't mean. He just…"

"Just what?" Mandy asked, effortlessly encouraging him. Which usually worked. People often opened up to her. It was a character trait that was destined to make her a star reporter one day.

"Alex didn't see me at all. It was like I was invisible to him, you know? So he never said hi or anything." Kyle glanced into the rear-view mirror to look at Mandy and shrugged. "But he didn't say anything mean around me either."

"So how many times did you see her before she went missing?" Mandy probed much more gently than Trent had. She'd probably learned a lot about interviewing witnesses from Jess, he figured.

"Only a couple of times. Her boyfriend drove them here from the airport in a Lambo. Nearly got them killed on the way." Kyle glanced into the mirror again. "Once the snow started really coming down, they couldn't take that thing anywhere, so I gave her a ride to the pharmacy in town one day."

Trent waited a beat to make sure Kyle was done talking before he asked, "Was she sick or something?"

"I don't think so. At least, not that she told me about. I didn't ask."

Trent sat back and chewed on that info for a while. The next half hour was a harrowing drive along roads almost snowed in during the last few storms. By the time they pulled off and headed toward a huge log cabin surrounded by trees, Mandy's cheeks were chalky. Trent was feeling slightly nauseated himself.

Kyle said, "Should be good skiing once it clears up, though.

Nothing like fresh powder." He pulled to the front of the building and popped the vehicle into park. He climbed out and unloaded their bags.

When they stood beside the Jeep and looked around, Mandy said quietly, "Maybe it's just the color of the sky, but the place feels creepier than I expected."

Trent had to agree. Sharp cold air combined with ominous clouds sent a sense of foreboding through him so strong he almost told Kyle to take them back to the airport.

But he'd come to do a job for one of his best law firm clients, one that could send a lot more business his way, too. He couldn't afford to leave until he'd finished. "Might as well get to work."

Mandy offered him a weak smile as they followed Kyle—now laden with their bags—through the wide, log doors. "I'm just glad to be off that road. A few times, I thought we were going to slide right over the edge and tumble down the mountain, didn't you?"

Behind the reception desk, a short, bald man waited, room key already in hand. Moving his small reading glasses to the tip of his nose, he surveyed the ledger. The waxed mustache was a little much, but he turned on a beaming, interested smile, so Trent let it pass.

"Welcome to the lodge." He handed the key to their driver. "To room 21B, please."

The kid nodded and headed up the wide, swooping stairs behind the desk with their bags.

"Kyle will take care of your things. Now, let's get you checked in, shall we?" He reached out a hand toward Mandy. "I'm Carl Asher, the manager here at Black Pines Lodge. It's a pleasure to meet you."

Mandy grinned. "Mandy Donovan. My pleasure. And this is Trent Brennan." She nodded toward him, and Trent offered his hand to the man who gave him a firm hand pump.

The check-in process went smoothly and, a few minutes later, Asher was stepping out from behind the desk.

"I'll show you to your room," Asher said, straightening his argyle sweater before guiding them toward the elevator. "So, what brings you to town? I hope you don't have gobs of exciting plans—looks like tonight's storm will be a doozy."

Trent cleared his throat. "So we've heard. No, we're mostly planning on getting some work done and relaxing a while. We might hit the slopes if the weather is good for it."

"This place is perfect for all of those things." The elevator dinged open, and Asher guided them down a long hall of gleaming hardwood and tasteful gold sconces. "What sort of work are you folks in?"

Mandy gave Trent the side-eye, probably wondering if he was going to tell everyone at the lodge exactly why they'd come since he'd already blabbed to Kyle.

"Investigative work on the Anderson case. Routine and not all that interesting. Rechecking some timelines and retracing some steps. On behalf of the family."

He didn't mention *which* family. He worried that people here at Black Pines had pre-judged Alex the way Kyle did, without having spoken a word to the guy. He wanted to avoid those roadblocks if possible.

Asher raised his eyebrows. "On the contrary, how fascinating." He slid the key into the silver card reader on the door and then swung it open for them. "Well, I won't keep you. If you need anything, all the numbers are beside the phone, and the reception desk is manned twenty-four hours a day. I don't expect to be busy with the storm coming, so you'll likely have my undivided attention."

Trent palmed him a ten-dollar bill. Asher tipped his head in thanks and added, "Hopefully I'll see you both later this evening. The bar is having a lovely happy hour special including two-for-one martinis and a brand new tapas selection."

Mandy smiled. "With any luck, we'll be there."

They closed the door and walked inside to find their bags waiting for them near the closet.

Mandy settled her hands on her hips sighed. "Well, we ought to get set up then, huh? Jess is on her way, and we've got a call in an hour so I can bring her up to speed. I have to read through the rest of the file, and I'd like to get a look at the area map again too. Or would you rather go out and explore the grounds a little?"

Trent pushed the thick, emerald curtains open to find a sky so dark it was almost menacing. "Looks like they weren't kidding about this storm. It's already started to snow."

The wind howled against the windows, doing the rest of the talking for him.

Mandy nodded. "Well, I don't know about you, but I'm stir-crazy and sick of being cooped up."

He nodded. "Okay, let's not hole up in here, then. Let's go mingle and see if we can get the gossip about Rebecca and Alex."

"Good plan." Mandy refreshed her make-up and changed her shirt. They headed down to the bar, the file secured firmly in her purse.

From the second they walked into the bar, their plans were thwarted. The place was practically deserted. A young couple was snuggled up in the corner who clearly did not want to be interrupted. The bartender was chatting away on the phone with his back to the room.

The place was cozy, though. Exactly the kind of ski lodge bar a tourist would expect, complete with crackling fireplaces and a mounted taxidermy moose head.

Mandy glanced at him, an unspoken question in her eyes, and he led her toward the bar with his hand on the small of her back.

"Bartenders tend to hear everything, even when people think they're not listening," Trent whispered.

She slid onto a stool beside him and shot her thousand-watt grin at the male bartender. It didn't take long for him to notice her.

"How can I help you guys?" He had Irish eyes and a quick and ready smile.

Trent cleared his throat. "She'll have a dirty Grey Goose martini, three olives and I'll have a Jack on the rocks, please."

"Coming up." The guy nodded, then set to work pouring and shaking and garnishing.

"Worked here long, Sean?" Trent asked, after reading the man's nametag.

Sean shrugged. "A couple years."

"So then, you heard about that missing girl, huh? Rebecca Anderson?" Trent asked, and Mandy shot him a look. He ignored her. He'd been a detective for a couple of years before he'd left Denver PD. The direct approach was often best. Might as well see if straightforward did the job here before overcomplicating things.

The bartender set two drinks in front of them. "Even if I knew anything about that, we're not permitted to discuss the matter with guests. I'm sorry." He frowned.

Trent took a sip of his drink. "I can understand that. But what if I told you we're not really guests?"

Mandy frowned and gave him the side-eye again.

"I don't think I follow." The bartender picked up a rag and started wiping down the bar, but Trent kept at him.

"I'm a private investigator here to look into what exactly happened to Rebecca, the missing girl. So, if there's anything you can share, it would really help us out."

The bartender's frown deepened, but he glanced around the bar furtively before leaning in close. "Look, I talked to the police. Can't they give that to you or something? I just don't want to get in trouble. They're real touchy about that whole thing. You can see this place is already a ghost town and it's not just because of the weather."

"There's nothing you can tell us that might help? There is a young woman missing who may still be alive out there somewhere and a lot of people would love to have her found safe." Mandy blinked up at him, and he let out an exasperated sigh.

"Okay, look." Sean glanced around again and then dropped his voice to little more than a whisper. "They—the couple I mean—came in for a nightcap late that evening. All I can say is, based on what I saw, she was furious with him. He kept trying to grab her hand and talk to her, but she wasn't having it. They argued, but I couldn't really hear what they were saying. After about twenty minutes, she got up and walked out. Said she was going back to the room and left him behind."

That wasn't news to either Mandy or Trent. The police report said as much. But as Mandy opened her mouth to ask a question, Trent reached for her hand and squeezed. Sean wasn't done talking yet. Trent could see it in his eyes.

"Look," he murmured conspiratorially. "I didn't mention this part to the police because it wasn't something I can say for sure...just a feeling, but he didn't seem bothered at all that she was crying. In fact, he was like...smirking when she left." He shrugged. "Anyway, I don't want that on the record. I'm just saying that was my feeling. He started tapping away on his phone and then, a few minutes later, he went upstairs."

Mandy gave Trent a significant look.

"Is that everything you know?" Trent asked.

The bartender nodded. "Like I say, I don't *know* anything. Only what I saw, and even that could mean nothing at all, right? But the girl was nice. I hope it helps."

Trent opened his mouth to thank him, but just as he was about to speak, another gust of wind battered the windows and made the whole place creak and moan. A second later, the soft music streaming from the speakers went quiet, and the lights flickered once.

Then, everything went dark.

CHAPTER THREE

ANOTHER *WHOOSH* OF WIND battered the windows and made the storm shutters whine as they sat in stunned silence.

Mandy reached for Trent, and though he gave her palm a reassuring squeeze, he knew it would do nothing to stop her hand from trembling in his. It was chilling as hell to be talking about a missing woman and have the lights die mid-conversation. The moon skittering off the snow provided some ambient light, but not near enough for his comfort level. He again found himself second-guessing his decision to take this job.

"Nothing to worry about," Sean said. "It'll take a minute, but the backup generator has never failed us yet."

Mandy let out a nervous chuckle and lifted her drink to her lips. The couple in the corner of the room fell silent. The only sound Trent heard was the continual moaning of the wind.

Finally, the slow, steady whining of the generator coming online filled the air as the lights came up and the drowsy jazz music poured from the speakers again.

"Just like I said." The bartender winked at Mandy.

"Great." Mandy turned to face Trent right as the wind cracked against the building so hard that the mounted moose head shifted on the wall and the room went dark and silent once more.

"Well, I suppose there's a first time for everything," Mandy said. Her usual good humor hadn't failed her yet, but Trent could hear it fraying around the edges, and he didn't blame her one bit. The place was creepy, just like she said. Even more so in the dark.

"Don't worry folks. I'm sure everything is under control, and it'll be handled right away. In the meantime, though," Sean reached beneath the bar and pulled out a long, thin flashlight. Flipping the switch, he placed the light just beneath his chin like he was going to tell a ghost story. "We can keep each other company. And, of course, drinks are complimentary for the duration of the outage."

Suddenly social, the couple in the corner sprang to their feet and ordered a fresh round from halfway across the room. Mandy glanced at them as they pulled up seats beside her, and though her face looked impassive, Trent felt her palm sweaty and shaky in his.

"You're not going to order another drink?" He raised his eyebrows at her as Sean swept by to light a candle on the bar-top.

"I don't want this one to get jealous," Mandy nodded to her half-full martini glass.

"You should have started worrying about making people jealous back when you were flirting with the bartender," Trent teased.

She rolled her eyes. "So you're the jealous type now?"

"Of course, I am. You never noticed?" But his teasing had dulled the shrill edge of fear in her voice. He tossed some money onto the bar and then helped her from her stool. "Probably better we keep our heads clear, anyway. Let's check the front desk and see what's going on."

Mandy nodded. "Okay, if that's the excuse you're going with."

When they reached the edge of the room, he opened the door for her and followed her into the hall. "Excuse?"

She shrugged. "All of a sudden you want to talk to the front desk? It has nothing to do with Sean the gallant bartender and your quest to protect my honor?"

Her blue eyes glanced at him from beneath a curtain of sun-kissed hair, and he squeezed her hand a little tighter. "Should I challenge him to a duel?"

"Maybe." In the dim moonlight skittering through the windows off the snow, he thought he saw her grin.

Just as he moved to pull her in for a quick kiss, another blast of wind crashed against the building, and she jumped. Leave it to Mandy to try to distract them from the reality of their situation. Her hand was trembling again, and he pulled her close, willing the power outage to end before they reached the lobby. Things had been strange enough with the ominous weather. Being stuck in the dark in the middle of nowhere during a blizzard gave new meaning the to the phrase "bad date."

"We'll light a fire when we get to the room," Trent offered, and Mandy nodded, looking relieved at the thought. Maybe with a fire and the moonlight they'd forget exactly how odd this power outage was. A lodge where a woman had gone missing only weeks earlier and the generator had never failed before.

At the reception desk, Asher looked dumbfounded. He was staring at his cell phone as if it had been struck by lightning.

"Everything okay, Carl?" Trent asked.

Asher shook his head, "Yes, yes, of course. Just waiting for the handyman. So sorry for the inconvenience." He flashed a tight smile.

Another gust of air battered the building, and this time Trent felt a distinctive chill skitter up the back of his neck.

"You'll want to stick to one of the rooms with a fireplace. Of course, your suite has one, but the bar and the veranda both have fires going, too. The heat is electric for the most part and, well—" Asher gestured around. "Obviously, that's going to take some doing."

"Of course," Mandy nodded and snuggled a little closer to Trent. "Fires are romantic as well as warm."

"I have a flashlight if you'd like me to lead you to your room and start a fire for you. I'm quite the expert."

Another gust of wind, this time positively icy, flooded the room and Trent turned around just as a hulking, snow-swept man in coveralls and a heavy winter coat trudged through the door looking like a Yeti.

"Evening," he said in a loud, booming voice. Trent distinctly heard Mandy let out a faint squeak.

The man unwrapped the snow-covered scarf to reveal a sculpted face, surrounded by a thick dark beard dotted with patches of gray. He rubbed his chin before nodding at Asher. "Came quick as I could. Storm's really whipping up fast."

Asher nodded. "I appreciate that." Gesturing for Trent and Mandy, he added, "This is Jim Kubiak, our handyman. He lives in the single cabin behind the lodge. He's a genius with this type of thing. Should be handled in no time."

Kubiak grunted his agreement. "Might as well get started. If you need me, I'll be out back." He lifted his scarf up again to protect his lungs from frostbite.

Trent's raised both eyebrows. "Are you really going out into the blizzard? You could freeze to death. Can't even see two feet in front of you."

Kubiak shrugged. "I've lived around here for years now. I'll be fine. Generator's up against the back of the lodge. Don't need to see. Just need to feel."

Trent frowned. "Let me go out there with you, hold the flashlight or whatever. You're going to need both hands to fix the generator."

"Absolutely not, sir," Asher said, shaking his head as Kubiak cut in.

"No, no, I can't ask you to do that." Kubiak's eyebrows caved into a scowl.

"Come on, man. I can't have you on my conscience," Trent said. "It'll make things even quicker if I help. Asher, if you don't mind, you could show Mandy up to the room and light the fire, and we'll be back before you know it."

"It's not the guests' responsibility to fix the generator. The owners wouldn't like it at all if they knew I allowed you to go out in this weather for that," Asher fretted, tugging at his mustache.

Trent adopted a conspiratorial tone. "Well then we won't tell them, will we, Carl?"

"I don't want you going out in this blizzard, either," Mandy grumbled, but Trent squeezed her shoulder gently.

"You've got a phone call to make, and I'm from Denver. I'm used to blizzards. Nothing to worry about. Be done before you know it. Back in a jiffy." Trent turned to the big man. "Come on, Jim, let's see if we can't save the day."

Asher led him to a closet full of coats they kept on hand for staff or guests who misplaced theirs, and Kubiak waited as Trent pulled on a coat and grabbed a flashlight.

Nodding to Mandy, he reminded her that he'd be right back and then headed off into the snow at the big Yeti's side.

CHAPTER FOUR

WHAT LITTLE CONVERSATION KUBIAK had to offer was lost in the howling wind and the torrent of snowflakes teeming down in an infinite white wall.

Trent kept his arm poised protectively in front of his face as he slogged through the mounds of ever-piling powder and followed Kubiak's barely visible silhouette.

"Much farther?" Trent asked. The big man grunted in response.

The generator was outside the back door of the lodge. A pair of cellar doors rested nearby, protected by an overhang and at an angle that kept them only lightly dusted with snow.

"All right, sooner we get this over with, the sooner we can warm up. I'm counting on you, Jim," Trent said, and Kubiak grunted again.

Aiming the flashlight where Kubiak directed, Trent moved to get a better angle. His boot slipped. He slid backward. A moment later, he hit an icy patch and toppled toward the snow-covered ground. He threw his hand out, desperate for purchase, waiting breathlessly for the cold, icy mound of deep snow to close around him.

Instead, he landed on something hard. Yet also kind of soft. And almost warm.

He scrambled backward and closed his fingers around the flashlight that had slipped from his hand.

He pointed the snow-dappled light at the thing that had broken his fall.

Dread clawed his throat.

His stomach pitched.

He stared at the familiar face.

"Rebecca," he gasped.

She was crammed into the space between the generator and the shed. Her body was covered in a few inches of new snow, save for the place where Trent had fallen on her and dislodged it.

"Kubiak," he called against the wind. When Kubiak turned his head, Trent called out, "We've got a problem over here."

Trent scrambled to his feet and moved toward Rebecca. He dusted the snow gently from her face with a quaking hand. Her eyes were closed, and no visible bruises so far as he could tell, although she wore a long-sleeved nightgown. He didn't see any blood, but most of her body was covered in snow.

"Well, shit," Kubiak grunted.

Moving closer, Trent pressed two fingers to her neck, searching frantically for a pulse. He felt nothing, but damn it, he knew she hadn't been out here long. Her skin was chilled, but not frozen, and her flesh was still soft and pliable.

He glanced at the shed and noted again the light dusting of snow around the door. He pointed to the doorframe. "They must have knocked the snow off when they brought her out here."

Kubiak frowned but made no comment. Trent's mind raced as he tried to think through the thick haze of cold, adrenaline, and surprise.

"Are there many homes nearby?" Trent asked. If the killer wasn't in the lodge now, it was possible that he was hiding someplace close. Someplace he didn't think he'd be caught while dumping Rebecca back here.

Kubiak shrugged. "Me and then about four of five other ski cabins in a two-mile radius."

"Where can we take her?" Trent gestured to Rebecca, but Kubiak's frown deepened.

"I get paid to fix the generator. That's what I'm going to do." He set back to work and Trent stared at him, baffled. Was he seriously going to crouch down in the snow and pretend he wasn't working a few inches from an injured woman? Was he some kind of sociopath?

Still stunned by the turn of events, Trent shined the flashlight into the surrounding snow. The only tracks were his and Kubiak's, which seemed to mean that whoever dragged her out here had come from inside the lodge's cellar.

Trent pinched the bridge of his nose and tried to stay calm. "The generator can wait. We need to get her back inside."

"Those fireplaces are built for ambiance, not warmth," Kubiak grumbled. "The whole place will be a meat locker inside of three hours if we don't get the heat going."

"We'll come back. After we get her inside. I can't carry her through this thick snow alone. Come on." Trent moved toward Rebecca and started to dislodge her from the space.

Kubiak's low growl interrupted him. "If she's dead, it's a crime scene. You can't go messing with—"

"If this is a crime scene, it's already a mess because we came trudging through before. There will be another two feet of snow covering it all before the cops ever get here anyway. They can't get to us in this weather. Attempting to come up that mountain road would be a suicide mission tonight. We've got to do something for her. We can't just leave her out here. I don't feel a pulse, but I don't see wounds, either. She might make it if we get her to a doctor right away."

He knew it was a long shot, but maybe the cold weather had helped slow her heartbeat down. Maybe there was a tiny chance... "While we're out here yammering, we could have her inside. We've got to try. A little help, Jim. Please."

Kubiak's face remained as impassive as ever, but after a long moment, he crouched over and helped Trent lift her from the snow.

Progress through the deep drifts into the wind was slow and painstaking. Trent slipped and fell twice. When they pushed through the lobby doors, they were both breathing hard.

They set her down on the area rug near the fireplace, and Trent knelt beside her, heedless of the gasps from the few hotel guests in the room. Vaguely, he could hear Kubiak explaining to someone what had happened. Trent tried again to find her carotid pulse using his cold fingers.

That was when he saw it.

On the side of her head, almost covered by her hair, was a small bullet hole slightly below her temple.

"She's dead." He looked up to find that he'd announced the truth not only to Kubiak, but also to Asher, Sean the bartender, and Mandy.

Everyone looked utterly stunned. Asher's face went white. Sean looked as though someone had struck him. Mandy's brow creased, intensely concerned. But then, Mandy had seen homicide victims before. Trent guessed the others had not.

Kubiak crossed his arms over his barrel chest. "Well, it's not like we didn't figure. Body don't go missing for a month and anything good come of it." He scrubbed at his bearded chin.

Trent got to his feet and took Mandy none-too-gently by the arm. "Please, let us know as soon as the authorities are contacted."

He pulled her toward the staircase, willing her to stay quiet with every step. Behind them, the staff murmured to each other about calling the police and their cell towers being down.

"What's the matter with you?" Mandy whispered, but Trent shook his head as he lit a pathway with the flashlight he still carried.

Trent pulled her up the staircase with him. She gave up the struggle and walked along.

When they were back in their room, he said, "Rebecca's been missing for weeks. The weather here has been below zero the whole time. But her body is still slightly warm. Definitely not frozen."

Mandy's eyes widened, and a hand flew to cover her mouth. Like Trent, she knew what that meant.

Whoever had killed Rebecca had done it today. Because of the blizzard, that could mean only one thing.

The murderer was almost certainly still here, in the lodge. Snowed in with everyone else.

Trent nodded. "Looks like the cheating young Alex Lloyd didn't kill her after all."

CHAPTER FIVE

"YOU COULD'VE BEEN KILLED," Mandy murmured, eyes wide as Trent finished explaining what had happened by the generator. "The murderer could've been right beneath your feet in that cellar, or even nearby, watching everything."

Neither of them said what they both were thinking. Rebecca's killer could've easily been Kubiak. He'd had opportunity enough. The question was, did he have a motive? He'd certainly been against the idea of Trent going outside to help with the generator.

"Were you able to reach Jess while I was gone?" Jess would know what to do, and from outside the lodge, she'd have a better chance to get the authorities up here as soon as the storm let up.

Mandy nodded. "I talked to her, but the connection was bad. I told her what was going on, but it's anybody's guess whether she actually heard me or not."

Trent pressed redial on his cell phone for the hundredth time, just hoping for a connection. The gods finally cut him some slack, and a ring tone sounded in his ear.

"Sheriff's Department."

"Hello? Hello, we're staying at the Black Pines Lodge, and we've just found the body of a dead woman outside in the snow. We believe it's Rebecca Anderson."

There was a muttered curse and then a long pause as static crackled over the line.

"Hello? Are you there?" Trent repeated into the phone. "This is Trent Brennan. Can you hear me?"

"Yes, sir, Mr. Brennan. I heard what you said, and I'm mighty sorry to get that news, but there's just no getting there until the storm breaks. The highways are all shut down, and this part of the state has declared a weather emergency. Even if I could get there on a snow machine using back roads, can't see your hand in front of your face out there."

Trent raked a hand through his hair and blew out his frustration. He'd known that would be the answer, but damn, it still made his blood run cold to hear it.

"Anything you can do to get here as soon as possible, please do it. I believe we found the body very shortly after her murder and I believe the murderer is likely still on the premises. We have no power here, and things are tense to say the least."

The connection faltered again, and all he heard was choppy pieces of a reply that he couldn't make out before the line went dead again.

He tossed the phone on the bed with a frustrated growl. "That girl is dead and the second this weather permits, the killer will have a chance to escape. I found her out there in the snow. How can I face her parents and tell them that I knew her killer was within these walls and I did nothing?"

Jess Kimball's words played in his head like a sermon. This wasn't about money or solving a case. This was about integrity and getting justice for Rebecca Anderson.

"While you were on the phone, I managed to get a text to go through to Jess. I gave her the name of the lodge and asked her to check if Jim Kubiak has a rap sheet. I also asked her to try to get a bead on Alex Lloyd and confirm his alibi." Mandy smiled. "She's on it, and, in the meantime, nothing we can do but sit tight."

"You're really good at this, you know?" He pulled her into his arms for a hug and then stepped back. "I'm going down to the cellar and look around. Before the killer has any more time to cover his tracks. Lock the door when I leave and then push this dresser in front of it, all right?"

She jerked back, and let out a crack of nervous laughter. "Have you lost your mind? Geez, it's like you've never seen a horror movie before. You don't split up, Trent. That's how you get your butt killed." She shook her head and pocketed her cell phone before picking up the flashlight. "We go together, or you don't go at all."

He studied the determined look in her eyes and the set of her jaw. No way was he going to win this argument. He could tell. The thought of putting her in harm's way made his gut twist. But when he opened his mouth to tell her she couldn't come along, the image of Rebecca's pale face and blue-tinged lips floated through his mind.

"It's okay," Mandy said softly. "I get it, and I'm a big girl. If I didn't think we should go, I'd be fighting you on it. Sometimes doing the right thing is hard and scary, that's all. But I'm in. Let's do this."

Trent made a mental vow to make everything up to her somehow once they got out of this mess.

If you get out of this mess.

He took a deep breath and silenced that naysaying inner

voice and ushered Mandy into the hallway on silent feet. He took the flashlight from her and extinguished it. She laced her fingers in his as they tiptoed down the front stairs using the walls to guide them.

As they reached the main floor, he strained to hear what the people in the lobby were saying, to no avail. The wind was still creating a cacophony that drowned out the murmured voices. Bad on the one hand, because he couldn't tell who was there and who wasn't. Good, because it masked the creaking floorboards as he and Mandy slipped past and skulked down the hallway toward what his usually reliable sense of direction said was the inside entrance to the cellar.

When they reached a door at the end of the hall, they both paused.

"Ready?" he whispered.

She didn't reply, but he could sense her nodding. He tugged on the doorknob, but it didn't budge.

He tried again, tugging harder. The third time, he planted both feet and leaned his full weight back on the handle. When it came swinging open, he and Mandy both stumbled back but managed to stay on their feet.

For a full thirty seconds, they stood at the top of the stairs, the eerie silence only broken by Mother Nature's wrath and the sound of their own harsh breathing.

No one came running down the hallway brandishing a flashlight or any other weapon, and his heart finally started beating again.

He put a hand on Mandy's arm and urged her to follow him. Once they were on the stairs, she closed the door behind them, and he turned on the flashlight.

If the killer were still down there, he'd hear them coming.

Trent gripped the heavy flashlight like a club. He peered into the darkness, in case the guy tried to rush them. Which was cold comfort as they descended the steps to the cellar.

The temperature dropped at least twenty degrees as they reached the bottom step. Their breaths made puffy white clouds in the air.

"Anyone here?" Trent called, moving the beam of the flashlight around the room in a slow, half-circle.

It was a standard basement, complete with cobwebs painting the ceiling and old tools littering the corners. A massive vice-grip sat on an ancient workbench against the back wall. A set of worn tractor tires formed a pillar beside it.

"Nothing?" Mandy whispered from behind him.

"Not so far." He stepped forward and scanned the room again. It was only then that he saw the wet boot prints on the cracked cement floor. A blast of adrenaline rushed through him as he shone the light to follow the boot prints. He paused when the prints stopped at the wall.

What the hell?

He crept closer, pulse knocking wildly. The boot prints ended not at a wall, but at a wooden panel leaning up against the wall. He gingerly lifted the panel aside with his free hand. Mandy gasped when the move revealed a narrow door with a latch on the outside.

He mustered every last drop of courage he possessed and slid the latch open with a *snick*. Then, he swung the door wide.

"Anyone in there?" he called, body tense and at the ready as he held the flashlight like a club.

He heard no shuffling or movement or sounds of human habitation. He stepped into the room and trained the light on the interior.

A single, stained mattress lay on the floor beside a rusty space heater. The dank smell he'd noticed in the main cellar was laced with the faint scent of human body odor. And something metallic he couldn't quite place.

After two passes with the flashlight, he found the source.

A pool of congealed blood on the floor right by his feet.

This was where Rebecca Anderson had been murdered. The blood wasn't even dry yet.

CHAPTER SIX

"MY GOD," MANDY WHISPERED as they both stared down at Rebecca's blood.

A macabre nightmare had come to life. The situation settled over him like a lead blanket.

Trent's mind raced as he tried to think of the next move. He knew he needed to alert someone on staff, but who could he trust? The only person he was sure of in this house of horrors was the woman standing beside him.

He was desperately trying to puzzle out the best course of action when Mandy's phone chirped. She flinched at the sound and then began rifling through her pockets until she found the glowing device.

"It's a text from Jess," she murmured as she thumbed down, scrolling over the lengthy message. "She's delayed due to the storm. And Alex Lloyd has a solid alibi tonight. He's in Denver at a retirement dinner for his dad. More than a hundred witnesses. She also made a couple of calls and, according to her sources, Jim Kubiak doesn't have a criminal record."

Her body tensed and he peered over her shoulder to read the rest of the text.

BUT, Carl Asher is listed as the manager there. He did prison time for sexual assault in '04. Dangerous. Help on the way. Be careful until cops arrive.

Carl Asher? The fussy desk manager with the silly mustache? Not possible.

Trent ran through the series of events that had led them here. He *had* told Carl about his investigation. And after he and Mandy went into the bar this afternoon, Asher had plenty of time to kill Rebecca.

The door at the top of the steps swung open, and footsteps sounded down the stairway.

Trent blinked, shielding his eyes as a high-powered flashlight sent his pupils into overload.

He blinked a few times and Asher came into view, gun first.

"Couldn't leave well enough alone, could you? Now I've got a mess on my hands."

Trent was about to do whatever it took to buy time, but Mandy was way ahead of him. She grabbed Trent's hand, shined the flashlight into Asher's eyes and let out an ear-piercing screech.

Asher didn't hesitate. He swung the gun wildly in Mandy's direction.

Trent acted on pure instinct.

He lunged forward and knocked the flashlight out of Asher's hand.

Asher fired, and the shot went wide, burying the slug into the wall a few feet from Mandy's head.

Asher let out a roar and ran at Trent like a bull.

Mandy flung the flashlight at his head.

The light flickered and went out as Asher howled in fury.

Trent lunged at him in the darkness.

The two men grappled while Mandy shouted for help, but her cries were lost in the noise of the storm.

Asher landed a vicious blow to Trent's solar plexus, and he bent over, temporarily stunned and breathless.

Asher acted on a dime, breaking away. The sound of footsteps echoed through the blackness as Trent tried to track his movements, but by the time he realized where Asher was headed, it was too late.

The cellar door by the generator swung open, and Asher launched himself out into the blizzard.

"Mandy, go upstairs and get Jim, Sean and any of the staff who are willing to help!" Trent shouted, sprinting toward the open cellar door. "If Kubiak doesn't get the generator going, set out flashlights in the snow around the lodge so I can find my way back."

"Don't go out there!" Mandy pleaded, scurrying after him and grabbing his hand. "He's not going to get far in this weather. He'll come back."

"Go up and tell the others what's happening. Put the flashlights out in the snow where I can see them." He pulled free and headed out into the blizzard. He called over his shoulder. "I'll be back soon."

The blinding snow was so thick that, even though Asher had only a thirty-second head start, he had disappeared.

Trent reached into his pocket for his cell phone. Only six percent battery left. He could use the phone's flashlight now or wait until he fought his way back. He'd rely on Mandy to light the way for his return.

He pressed the button, shining the phone's light toward the ground in front of him.

He saw Asher's tracks in the snow ahead, but the wind and fresh snowfall already had wiped them out in places. Trent moved forward in slow, lurching steps, following Asher's path like a trail of birdseed.

"Come on, Asher," he called out into the white abyss. "You'll die out here in the cold."

He didn't expect a response, and he didn't get one. But he trudged on. Already, his fingertips were numb, and his limbs sluggish. How long could he resist hypothermia, he wondered, even as he walked farther from the lodge's warmth.

The cold bit relentlessly. The barrage of icy snowflakes stung his cheeks, his hands, and every inch of his exposed flesh. His lungs hurt with exertion and each sharp inhale of frigid alpine air.

Still, he pressed on. Every minute or so, he shot a glance back the way he'd come. He could no longer see the lodge, or anything except blinding snow in all directions. He faced forward in the whiteout.

All he could do was focus on the task at hand or lose himself to panic.

Find Asher.

Set one foot in front of the other.

He repeated the words in his mind, eyes trained on the ground in front of him, trance-like, until he realized that Asher's tracks were no longer covered over with fresh snow.

Something had happened. He was closing the gap, and quickly.

His heart raced as he caught sight of a small dark shape in the snow, a few feet ahead. He plunged toward it, a sense of triumph coursing through him.

A man's boot, wedged in a deep drift of hard-packed snow.

"I know you're close Asher," he called loudly, projecting his voice to carry over the blustering wind. "You'll lose that bare foot to frostbite. You've got to get indoors. Let's end this now. There's nowhere to go from h——"

Trent's words were cut short. Movement in his periphery jerked him to a halt. He barely had time to brace himself as Asher rushed from his blind side, taking him to the ground like a linebacker.

"You c-crazy bastard," Asher stammered with cold. He gripped Trent's coat in his fists and slammed his body against the soft snow. "You don't even know that girl, and now you're going to die for her."

Trent's head landed hard on a rock. His vision blurred as a white-hot shaft of pain split through his skull. He tried to focus on what Asher was saying, but his mind felt scrambled.

Asher reached to his waistband with one hand, closed his fingers around Trent's throat with the other, and squeezed.

Blackness closed in around him, and he fought it with everything he had.

In the distance, perhaps from the lodge, he heard a single gunshot. Another. Had Mandy sent Kubiak to rescue him?

Trent mustered all his strength and used his size to his advantage. He rolled hard to the right. The move sent Asher toppling off him into the snow. Asher's gun went flying.

Trent clambered to his feet. He nearly lost his balance as nausea swept through him. But he pushed forward and bent to jerk Asher to his feet.

The smaller man had the strength of a wolverine. He fought wildly, fists flying in a flurry of punches to Trent's face and stomach.

In their scuffle, Trent's still-illuminated cell phone skittered across the snow.

As he defended himself against Asher's attack, he strained to use the weak blue light to find Asher's gun.

He gasped. His cell phone sat precariously on the edge of a cliff just two yards away.

Asher fought so hard because he knew the cliff was there.

Trent realized they were on the very edge of the mountain and, for the first time, he fully understood that one of them would die.

Asher sent his elbow crashing into Trent's nose. The move blinded him as his eyes teared and searing agony shot through his whole face. Reflexively, he released his hold on Asher.

Trent wiped his eyes with his forearm. When he could finally see again, he looked at Asher. Three few feet in front of him. Gun in hand.

"Time's up, superhero."

Trent swallowed hard. "Everyone knows it's you, Asher." He swiped at the hot gush of blood running from his battered nose with his sleeve. "You can go down for one murder or two. But you're not getting out of here."

Asher grinned, breathing heavily, his neatly waxed mustache covered in white powder above stained yellow teeth. "You'd be surprised what I manage to get away with. Hell, I kept that girl on this mountain for a month, and no one was the wiser. Cops in and out, even the family came one weekend."

Trent fought the urge to rush forward and knock them both over the edge.

Keep him talking.

"How? How did you do it?"

"My family has a fishing cabin a couple of miles away. I was keeping her there, but then the blizzard was brewing. I was afraid I wouldn't be able to get to her if we got snowed in at the lodge and she'd freeze to death." Asher shrugged. "So I drugged her and carried into the cellar. The lodge was almost empty anyway. Figured she'd keep and once the weather cleared, I'd take her back. But then you showed up. It's your fault she's dead, you know."

A wave of rage rushed over Trent. "Yeah. Without me, then what? You could've kept her as a prisoner in your cabin forever?"

"Well, until I got sick of her at least. But what's done is done." Asher's trigger finger moved slowly in the cold, but his intention was clear.

An eerie sense of calm settled over Trent. One good thing about being numb with cold. The bullet would hurt a lot less.

He let out a roar and dove sideways at Asher in a football move he remembered from college.

"Trent!" Mandy's scream came from the direction of the lodge.

Followed by a gunshot the distance.

Asher had doubled over a moment before his twitchy finger pulled the trigger. His gunshot cracked through the night air, echoing through the valley.

The hard shot to Trent's shoulder pushed him back.

Instinctively, he released Asher as he fell, slapping his free hand to his shoulder.

Asher's hands scrabbled at Trent's arm, trying to hang on even as Trent's body jerked back.

Asher stumbled, blood blooming on his torso where the first gunshot had hit him.

Trent landed hard on his back into the snow.

Asher lost his balance. He tumbled backward into the abyss of darkness. His bloodcurdling scream went on for long seconds before it stopped.

The only sound Trent heard was Mandy calling out as she ran. "Trent! Trent!"

It was only then that his shoulder exploded into a hot poker of agony.

He closed his eyes. It was cold...so damned cold.

He'd been wrong.

The cold hadn't numbed him at all. His shoulder hurt like hell.

CHAPTER SEVEN

"I THINK HE'S WAKING up." Mandy's quiet voice seeped through the humming in his ears as a shaft of light breached the darkness.

He blinked again and winced.

He'd heard the term "everything hurts" before, but this was the first time he could honestly say he knew what it meant. Even his rattled teeth ached.

But he was alive.

He felt a warm hand on his and turned his head to see Mandy and Jess standing beside the bed.

Mandy's eyes were bright with unshed tears and she grinned at him. "Man oh man, you gave me a scare."

"Yeah," he murmured, "I gave myself a scare too. Where are we?"

"We're at the hospital in Wyoming about an hour from the lodge. The storm ended and Jess got a helicopter to transport you."

His brain barely made sense of her words.

Mandy's smile faltered, and it looked like she was about to start crying, but she pushed through. "You were shot in the chest,

Trent. The bullet lodged about a quarter inch from your heart. They had to go in and get it and then patch you up."

His mouth felt like he'd been eating cotton. "Asher?"

Mandy cast her eyes down, but she kept her hand on his arm.

"He landed at the bottom of the mountain. If the gunshot didn't kill him, there's no chance he survived the fall." Jess cleared her throat. "If it wasn't for Mandy's marksmanship and quick thinking, you'd be dead and he'd be gone."

"You came after me?"

Mandy nodded and squeezed his hand. "Of course."

He thought back to the night on the mountain and frowned, sending a shaft of pain through his head. "Wait…how did I even get back? The last thing I remember is pushing Asher after he shot me and then…nothing."

Mandy released his hand and busied herself pouring him about an inch of water in a plastic cup. "Some of us were able to get you back to the lodge is all."

Jess shook her head and shot Mandy an exasperated glance. "My fabulous assistant here is being too modest. She spearheaded a search party. She and Jim Kubiak essentially dragged you back on a makeshift stretcher."

He whispered, "You could've been killed, Mandy."

She waved him off, cheeks flushed. She held a cup of water with a bendy straw so he could sip. "Jim tied what felt like a hundred ropes together, and we had lots of flashlights. It was no big deal."

But it had been a very big deal. Guilt settled in his gut as he thought of Kubiak. Big, quiet guy, a little weird and he'd automatically suspected him. As brave as Mandy had been, almost to the point of foolishness, she couldn't have carried him back alone.

"I sent him a huge gift basket of coffees and baked goods. When you're better, you can thank him yourself," Mandy murmured, reading his mind.

He cleared the emotion from his voice with a cough. "And what about Asher? Do the police have everything they need? He confessed to killing Rebecca if they need a statement."

"They will, eventually." Jess nodded. "But the bullet they dug out of your chest matched the one that killed Rebecca. Asher dropped the gun out there, and they found it, too."

He closed his eyes. "Good."

Mandy said, "Once they got into the lodge and his cabin, turns out you may have stopped a serial murderer, Trent. There was evidence tied to at least two other murders."

He nodded. He'd been too late to save Rebecca, but saving others was something to cling to. He nodded weakly.

"You did a good job here, Trent," Jess patted his arm. "Get some sleep. When you're better, I might have a bit of work for you."

He managed a smile for her. Now, all he had to do was make this all up to Mandy. He gestured, and she bent over to hear him. "So, I'm thinking our next trip should be Hawaii maybe…"

THE END

FATAL
PAST

CAST OF CHARACTERS

Jessica Kimball
Sam Sommers
Melinda McAllister
Trina Rickland

CHAPTER ONE

GOOD THING I'M NOT claustrophobic, Sam Sommers thought
again as he listened intently to the tour guide. The underground
tunnel system of centuries-old stone corridors known as the
Mines of Paris was damp and close, but also fascinating.

Sam shuffled along with the group, resisting the urge to
explore on his own. The tour guide had warned them several times.

The tunnel system was complex, Pierre had said. It was easy
to get lost, even in the subset of the network known as the
Catacombs of Paris. Some passages were narrow and had low
ceilings. Cave-ins weren't common, but they weren't rare, either.
There were good reasons why wandering the tunnels without an
official escort was illegal, and had been since 1955.

Not that Sam planned to wander around on his own. He
wasn't claustrophobic, but he had no desire to be lost
underground forever, either. The mere thought of it sent a shot of
electricity through his body. He grimaced. Maybe he was a touch
claustrophobic after all.

A few feet ahead, the group had stopped to hear more of
Pierre's expertise.

"Then, in the 1800s, the haphazard collection of bones was moved to the care of Louis-Étienne Héricart de Thury. He was tasked with making the underground graveyard into a mausoleum that could be visited by the public." Pierre spoke in hushed tones, reverently, as a priest might describe the Holy land.

Pierre's English was heavily accented, too. Sam had had trouble understanding him from the beginning of the tour. He squinted and leaned in as if those actions would improve Pierre's delivery or Sam's own comprehension. Nope.

"As you can see, those nineteenth-century efforts resulted in the haunting walls made of skulls and femurs that you see today. The history in these walls is breathtaking, and this tour barely scratches the surface. Beneath the Paris streets run many more miles of twists and turns." Pierre swept his arm out wide with a flourish before dropping his voice to a near whisper. "Who knows what secrets are hidden within the depths of the mines?"

"Spooky," said the man standing next to him.

Sam shot a grin to the fellow at his side and nodded in agreement. "Yeah, Pierre's really selling it, isn't he?"

Despite the guide's over-the-top performance, Sam found the catacombs pretty amazing. He thought of the magnitude of the underground beneath the city and shook his head in awe.

See, this was what he'd come to France to do. Granted, he had started slowly. This was his first vacation in more than twenty years, not counting a couple of weekend trips to Vegas for one buddy or another's bachelor party.

He'd planned a trip filled with exploration and new experiences, things he'd stubbornly resisted pretty much his whole life. Or, at least, that's what his ex-wife said when she divorced him.

Once he'd made the long journey and settled into his swanky room, though, his adventurous spirit abandoned him.

He'd spent more time exploring the patisseries and sampling the cheeses than exploring the city. He already had an extra inch around the waist to show for it.

He made a mental note. Tomorrow the choice between stuffing his gullet with fine wine and creamy Gruyère atop a crusty baguette, or ambling around the cobbled streets looking for history and culture would come around again. He vowed to remember how cool these tunnels were and get off his butt.

His stomach grumbled, and he almost laughed out loud.

Maybe there was a happy medium. He was here for another two weeks and then it was straight from a three-week "retirement" from the Denver Police Department to running his own private security firm. If he let himself go too much, he'd find himself lacking clients. Nobody wanted an overweight, out of shape ex-cop protecting them, after all.

Or so he assumed. He'd never worked private security full time. He didn't know what those pampered rock stars and teen idols wanted. But he would soon find out.

That settled, he focused again on the wall he'd been studying. A few minutes later, he realized that the majority of the group had followed the guide further away, down a short corridor.

"I'd love to bring my daughters here."

Sam turned and glanced again at the British guy who had been chatting with him on the bus and through much of the tour. Rory, he'd said his name was.

"Why didn't you?"

Rory shrugged. "I couldn't afford to make the jaunt when they were younger. Now they're both living in the States, so I really can't afford it."

"Yeah, I have a couple kids myself. A daughter in college and a son who is married. I think they'd love it here. My son, especially." Sam nodded. "He's an engineer."

"My daughters are both married, too," Rory replied with a snort. "That's the thing of it. I'd manage flying them out here, but they'd want their worthless husbands to come. Not on my dime."

Sam didn't want to weigh in on any of that. If he'd wanted family drama, he'd have his own. He tugged out his little pamphlet to check the map.

He pointed. "Looks like they're headed this way. Let's catch up, so we don't miss anything."

Rory fell into step beside him, but as they passed a tunnel blocked off by a rusted, metal door, Sam slowed.

"Do you smell that?" he asked, sniffing the air.

"Smell what? I've been smelling musty, moldy scents since we started," Rory replied.

Sam stopped abruptly.

Not possible. Surely, he had to be mistaken. After thirty minutes immersed in old bones, his imagination must have kicked in. But as he moved closer to the rusty door, the odor became unmistakable.

A smell he'd hoped never to encounter again after he'd retired.

One that had filled his days and haunted his nights for two decades. Surely, he'd had enough already.

He squeezed his eyes closed and mentally ran through his options. He could call the guide back and tell Pierre his suspicions. But that would cause a panic when he wasn't even a hundred percent sure himself.

Or he could roll up his sleeves and check it out. He was probably wrong, anyway.

He shrugged and approached the twisted metal door. He tugged once, and then again, harder, half hoping it wouldn't give. Then the decision would be out of his hands.

At first, the hinges held, but then the metal opened with a screeching squeal. If the gate had ever been sealed tight, it had been pried open recently. Which amped his radar up from orange to full red alert.

"You're not supposed to go in there, I don't think," Rory said, his tone stiff.

One hundred percent correct. But with the door opened, the unmistakable odor intensified. The last of Sam's doubts scattered.

"Rory, can you do me a favor and run up ahead and alert the tour guide to get everyone topside ASAP? Once he's done that, have him call the police immediately."

Rory stared at him, nonplussed. "What's going on, mate? Are you having a stroke or something? Do you smell almonds? Because my wife is a nurse, and she says—"

"Please," Sam cut in, keeping his voice calm and cool. "I'm fine. This is important. Please do as I ask, all right?"

Rory's full head of dark hair bobbed up and down, but his mouth was still flapping. "Right, then. But can you just tell me what's going on?"

Sam managed to hold back a frustrated growl as dread washed over him. "I'm afraid there is a dead body behind this gate."

Rory smiled. "Haven't you been listening to Pierre? There's dead bodies everywhere. This is a sacred burial ground."

Sam frowned. "If I'm right, this body is much more recent."

Rory's eyebrows lifted, and his mouth formed a startled "O." He turned and hurried to catch up with Pierre while Sam stood guard.

CHAPTER TWO

FOR THE NEXT COUPLE of hours after the Paris *Police Nationale* arrived on the scene, Sam answered questions and then stood aside while the body of a young woman was located and removed from the cave behind the metal door.

Apparently "translator" had a looser definition in France. Or, at least, that was what Sam assumed as he tried to decipher what the woman standing beside the detective was saying.

Vaguely, he recognized her words as English. But her accent was so thick that he caught himself leaning toward her as if that might help him understand better, which was no more effective with her than it had been with Pierre. While he'd tried to bone up a little on his French for the trip, he'd only mastered the basics, which definitely didn't include "mummified cadaver" or pretty much any of the words he'd have needed to discuss the situation.

"Thank you very much for your aid," the translator said. "You may now return to your life with the understanding that you will make yourself available should the police require more questioning. This is your correct hotel address?"

She held out a slip of paper with the address neatly scrawled on it, and he nodded.

"Very well, thank you again."

It took him a moment to realize he'd been dismissed. After he had processed the words, he glanced at Rory and tilted his head toward the exit.

Rory trailed him back onto the cobblestones streets. Even though the soft late afternoon light bathed everything in a comforting glow, Sam thought only of that poor, dead girl with the faded tattoo, carried past him on a stretcher.

Perhaps the partially mummified body had been too fragile to risk lifting into a body bag. They'd covered her with a sheet that succumbed to a stiff breeze once they climbed the winding steps. He should've looked away, but he'd been frozen in place. Now, he couldn't scrub the image from his mind. He imagined the indelible image was even worse for poor Rory.

"You all right?" Sam asked, and Rory nodded.

"Another vacation story, I suppose." Rory's strained smile flitted across his pale face. "Where are you headed?"

Sam nodded in the direction of his hotel.

Rory shrugged. "I'm the opposite way. Perhaps I'll see you 'round."

"Maybe," Sam agreed.

Rory started off and Sam did the same. His bones felt heavy as he trudged toward his hotel. Maybe instead of trying to pretend nothing had happened, he should take a few minutes to let it sink in and then take a nap or a hot shower. Anything to get himself to stop thinking about the girl.

He made his way up to his room, mentally listing all the things he still wanted to do on this trip. There was the Louvre and the Eiffel Tower. Lots of tourist attractions in Paris. A brasserie he'd seen on his way to the catacombs earlier had looked pretty good.

The thought of food turned his stomach, and again the image of the girl's leathery skin and gaping mouth filled his head.

Stop.

The police were on it. They knew what to do from here—how to conduct themselves and, hopefully, find justice for that Jane Doe. Though, of course, if that were true, maybe her body would have been discovered long before he'd found it.

How had no one smelled her before? Granted, it wasn't the usual funk of a long-dead corpse. Clearly, some sort of preservation process had taken place in the underground air, but still. Even among the dust and bones, he'd recognized the smell. Anybody with experience would have noticed it.

He pushed through his hotel door and made straight for the bed. He shoved the comforter aside before tucking himself beneath the covers, shoes and all. He was exhausted, weary.

He just needed to close his eyes.

But whenever he did that, there she was again. With that strange quote tattooed on her clavicle—

Oh world, you're too beautiful for anyone to realize you.

Now, with the adrenaline gone and in the quiet of his hotel room, he realized the quote felt oddly familiar. He sat up in bed and grabbed his laptop from the nightstand. He just needed to see. Where had he heard the quote before? After he answered that question, he'd be able to sleep and regroup.

Swiftly, he typed the words into a search bar, and the result popped up—the words came from a famous play.

Our Town.

If he recalled, that play was very specifically about life in America. Come to think of it, if the girl had been French, he wouldn't have been able to read the tattoo at all.

Why hadn't that occurred to him at the scene?

He tacked on the word "tattoo" to his search term on the laptop and refreshed the page.

Nothing other than the quote appeared on the first page. He flipped through two more pages until the answer he was looking for popped. A news headline. *Missing Co-Ed Presumed Dead.*

Beside the stark declaration was a picture of the girl's face.

Except it wasn't her face. At least, not the face he'd seen. She wasn't mummified and horrible. Her mouth twisted open in a ghastly scream. She was young and beautiful, with thick blond hair and bright hazel eyes. She was grinning at the camera and pointing to a mottled, newly-minted tattoo, the swirling script shiny with anti-bacterial ointment.

Let it go, Sam.

But he couldn't let it go. Swallowing hard, he clicked on the article and skimmed.

It was from an American gossip paper, dated on the one-year anniversary last year.

The American college student, Melinda McAllister, reported missing a year ago this past Saturday is probably dead, French officials say. After a lengthy and search and diligent investigation, authorities have found no trace of the missing young woman.

The disappearance of Melinda McAllister was strange right from the start. The more we learned about the situation, the stranger the story became.

McAllister was in Paris for several months, studying abroad. Her roommate, Trina Rickland, attended the same college. Rickland said McAllister left late in the afternoon and never returned home on that Thursday evening.

Rickland did not report McAllister's disappearance to officials. After her absence was noticed by fellow students, Rickland was questioned by authorities and admitted McAllister was gone. The timing and other circumstances cast immediate suspicion on Rickland.

Neighbors said they heard a terrible fight between the girls earlier in the day. Traces of McAllister's blood were found in the apartment.

Although Rickland was questioned about the fight, she was not arrested.

A source from Taboo Magazine reported conversations with other students. According to those who knew her, Rickland would never have harmed McAllister. It was said that the two were close friends. Many students used the same word to describe the two: "inseparable." Too inseparable, perhaps.

After McAllister had disappeared, reporters learned additional facts reflecting a strange relationship between the two women. They had recently received matching tattoos, quoting two lines from Our Town, the famous Thornton Wilder play. Rickland had changed her college major to the same as McAllister's English studies. Rickland and McAllister planned to rush the same sorority following their return to the United States.

Most chilling were the dozens of images found in Rickland's possession, showing McAllister in her most private moments. Many of the photographs were obviously snapped without McAllister's knowledge.

In a lengthy feature article at the time, Taboo Magazine Reporter Jess Kimball, suggested caution, mentioning Rickland's explanations for her behaviors. For example, Rickland incredulously said the images were her attempts to practice

*candid photography. She said McAllister had granted permission
for the photos.*

*Kimball's report on McAllister's disappearance said,
"Young girls often copy each other. Trina is distraught and
worried. She's fully cooperated with authorities and turned over
every rock looking for Melinda. Remember, no evidence exists to
prove that Trina is in any way responsible for her friend's
disappearance."*

*While Kimball's observation may be true, McAllister's
friends say Rickland was obsessed with McAllister, and this is a
case of obsession gone horribly wrong.*

The article continued in a similar style, repeating more
salacious details and conjecture, until Sam could read no more
and clicked it closed. He was disgusted by the sensationalized,
biased reporting branding Trina Rickland guilty of murder
without a shred of proof. He shook his head. The gossip rag had
glommed onto the tawdriest possible conclusions simply to move
copies, and that always irritated him to no end.

He did some more snooping among the hits from his search.
He read the well-written and researched piece written by Jess
Kimball. And then he looked for more, scouring the internet until
he felt wired.

Sleep was out of the question. Now that he'd started on the
Melinda McAllister case, he couldn't seem to stop.

You're retired, remember? A little voice bleated in his mind.
But he shoved it back as he calculated the time difference. After
a couple of attempts, he located his cell phone under the bed
where he'd accidentally kicked it. He found the number in his list
of contacts and placed the call.

"Jess Kimball speaking."

Her voice was still familiar to him, though it had been years since they'd spoken. She was young back then when her son was taken from her apartment. Sam had caught the case when the first call came into the station, and he'd never forget it. She'd been sobbing so uncontrollably that he couldn't make out her words at first. The case never got any easier.

Sam had found her to be both intelligent and tenacious. Excellent qualities for an investigative reporter, but heartbreaking for a mother whose son Sam had never found.

She'd followed up with him regularly for the first few years. But after a while, he no longer had the heart to comfort her tortured soul. He wasn't proud of it, but he'd made excuses to avoid her until she stopped calling.

Which didn't mean he'd stopped looking for Peter. Quite the opposite. Sam tried everything, without success.

He'd found Peter's open case file in his desk drawer when he'd cleared his stuff out of the Denver P.D. headquarters. He'd stared at the folder a good long time. Finally, he left it there, square in the middle of the desktop. Maybe his replacement would succeed where Sam had failed.

"This is Jess Kimball," she said again. "How can I help you?"

He pushed his voice past the lump in his throat. "Hey Jess, this is Sam Sommers from Denver P.D."

Her breath caught. "It's been a while." Wary. Tentative.

He winced. He'd been so focused on the McAllister girl that he hadn't considered how she'd react to hearing from him out of the blue after all these years. "I'm sorry, Jess. I'm not calling about Peter. I wish I did have something to tell you there, but my call is about something else."

"I see." She seemed to breathe a little easier, even over the wireless signal across the miles. "How can I be of service to D.P.D. today?"

He put a smile into his voice. "Actually, I just retired. Still not quite sure how I feel about it."

"Oh, well, in that case, congratulations." She waited, maybe a little distracted, probably hoping he'd come to the point and hang up.

"Thank you," he hedged, suddenly unsure. Maybe he shouldn't drag Jess into his mess this time. This felt like his last chance to walk away before the poor girl's case swallowed him completely.

But he couldn't do it. Not after he'd seen pictures of Melinda's face the way it had been when she was alive. So full of light and promise. So like his own daughter.

"Sam? Are you still there? I'm on deadline here, and I've only got a couple more minutes."

"Yes. Sorry." He coughed. "I'm taking some time off before I officially open a private security firm, and decided to come to Paris."

"Well deserved, I'm sure." Now she definitely seemed preoccupied.

He coughed again and then got right to it before he lost her interest. "Problem is, it seems I've found myself on the job again, in a sense."

"Oh?" Her voice lilted, and he hoped he'd set the hook.

"I went on a tour of the catacombs and happened on an unsolved homicide." He went on to explain the way he'd found the girl and described the body. He followed with a brief report about his interactions with the police. Finally, he got around to Jess's articles about the missing girl he'd read online. "What with Melinda McAllister going missing in Paris and the tattoo with the same quote, it's probably her."

"Oh, Sam. I'm sorry to hear all of that." Jess's solemn tone carried across the miles. "I'm still not sure why you're calling, though."

Sam cleared his throat. "Since you covered the case back when it first happened. I was hoping you might be able to tell me something about the roommate, Trina Rickland, or Melinda McAllister that wasn't in your articles. Something that might help find her killer."

"Well, everything was covered extensively by the news media at the time. The basic story was that Melinda seemed to have had a great life and a bright future. No one knew what happened to her. She simply disappeared." Jess paused for a few moments. He heard a clicking keyboard. "I was still hoping she was alive. After all this time, I suppose your news is not too surprising."

Sam nodded, although she couldn't see him. "And what about Rickland? Anything there that might help?"

Jess sighed. Sam pictured her running her fingers through her curly blonde hair like she often did. "Well, I defended Trina at the time because the story needed balance. I'd met her and talked to her, and I didn't believe she had harmed Melinda. She seemed as bewildered as everyone else. Most of my colleagues in the press disagreed with me. Their theory was that Trina was obsessed with Melinda and killed her in a fit of jealous rage."

"Was there any evidentiary support for that theory at the time?"

"None that I remember. I'm just looking through my notes." Jess paused again, murmuring as if reading quickly. "Right. They found no body. Only a few traces of Melinda's blood in the apartment. Not enough to suggest a serious wound. Witnesses said they'd been arguing the day before Melinda took off, but no one reported arguing that Thursday."

Sam said, "Sounds like the whole thing was a witch-hunt. Basically, Trina Rickland was a convenient and juicy suspect. She was tried and convicted in the court of public opinion, even if she was never charged with a crime."

"Exactly. The way they framed it, Melinda was the perfect student with a choirboy quarterback boyfriend and a solid, supportive family. Trina didn't have any of that. Far from it. She was a poor kid. On scholarship. No family at all. She started hanging around Melinda, emulating her, and Trina's life seemed to get better. She was like a puppy, following Melinda around." Jess took a quick breath. "Well, you can imagine how the gossip mongers painted everything when Melinda disappeared. Trina's accusers were loud and harsh. I wanted to believe she wasn't to blame."

He frowned. "You sound like you've changed your opinion."

"Trina's had a tough time in life, and Melinda's disappearance only made things worse. Now that Melinda's body has been found, the press will be all over Trina again. Such a shame." The keyboard clicking stopped, and Jess cleared her throat. "Yes, here it is. I didn't put this in my article at the time because I couldn't confirm it. I don't think anyone else mentioned this, but what I wrote down is just as I remembered. Both girls toured those catacombs about a week before Melinda disappeared."

"Melinda's body was found in a place that they'd recently visited together?" His tone was incredulous, and he shook his head.

"Could go either way, I guess," Jess said, tentatively.

"Meaning what?"

"If someone wanted to cast even more suspicion on Trina, hiding Melinda's body in the catacombs would have accomplished the goal." Jess took a breath and let it out in a long sigh. "On the other hand, it feels too suspicious. More like a frame-up."

Sam considered the possibilities and made no reply.

"I hope I didn't make a mistake about Trina," Jess said. "Maybe my colleagues were right after all."

"Doesn't feel right to me. Why don't you come over here, bring your notes, and help me dig out the truth?" Sam could hardly believe he'd said that. He was retired. His homicide investigation days were supposed to be behind him.

Her breath caught. He raised his eyebrows. He hadn't meant to suggest it, but he couldn't take it back.

"I don't want to get mired in this situation again," Jess said.

He pushed forward. This phone call was costing him a fortune. Might as well make the most of it. "Trina is more likely to get a fair shake if you're here."

There was a long silence over the line. He waited. If she was the same woman he'd known all those years ago, she'd reach the right decision without any further prodding.

Finally, Jess said, "I need to meet my deadline. Afterward, I'll reschedule a couple of things and check flights. I can probably get there tomorrow. Let me take down your number."

"Call me when you have your arrival info, and I'll pick you up at the airport. Meanwhile, I'll see what I can find out." He clicked off and resettled into the desk chair.

He opened his laptop again and scrolled to a new picture, this one of Trina and Melinda arm in arm near the Champs-Élysées. They looked like fraternal twins. Not identical, but close enough. Same hair style, same color. Same clothes.

Like everyone said, the resemblance was eerie, right down to the lip-gloss. Had the tabloids been right? Had Trina become obsessed with Melinda and killed her? But for what reason? He shook his head. That theory made zero sense.

He wasn't a Denver P.D. detective anymore, but he felt the familiar pull of an unsolved case, a new investigation. He and Jess Kimball were not so different in that way. Neither one could ignore the chance to make things right.

His brain was buzzing and his body vibrated with the need to hit the streets and dive in headfirst.

Screw rest and relaxation.

Now he was on the case.

CHAPTER THREE

BY THE TIME JESS arrived late the next afternoon, Sam had worked himself into a fine lather. He'd studied every detail he could find about both Trina and Melinda. He'd traced their social media profiles to see what they'd posted around what he estimated as the time of the murder. Six days after their visit to the catacombs. The day Melinda disappeared.

If Trina and Melinda had really visited the catacombs together, neither of them had posted about it. In fact, neither girl had posted anything at all on the day Melinda went missing.

A week after Melinda's disappearance, Trina's Facebook page went completely silent. But Melinda's was flooded with sympathy tributes and heartfelt testimonials about her life.

Jess knew the case way better than Sam did. He was counting on her to help him uncover the truth.

Sam collected Jess from the airport. They didn't bother to stop at her hotel but headed straight for the police station.

"Have you heard anything from the locals?" Jess had reviewed everything on the flight over and was ready to roll.

Sam shook his head. "Not a word. I know they're still in

possession of the body, but that's it. They basically told me to mind my own business, and they'd handle the case."

Jess blew a deep breath out through her nose and said nothing more. When he parked in front of the station, she hurried from the car to the entrance, leaving him to follow briskly behind her.

When they reached the desk, Jess asked in rushed, stilted French if the woman behind the counter spoke English.

"Oui." She nodded. "How can I help you?"

"I'm Jess Kimball." Jess handed the woman her *Taboo Magazine* business card. *Taboo* had a Paris office, and the magazine was as well known here as it was in the states. She waited while the woman examined the card as if it was radioactive. "I'm here to speak with Detective Lacroix, please."

"Impossible." The woman shook her head. "Lacroix retired six months ago."

Jess chewed on her lower lip and seemed to consider her reply before responding. "Can you put me in touch with the lead investigator in the Melinda McAllister case? I understand a body was recovered yesterday that might be Melinda's. I covered the matter when she first went missing. I'd like to help."

The woman punched out a number on the telephone and then spoke with someone on the other line in rapid French. Still holding the receiver, she frowned up at Sam. "And you are?"

"Sam Sommers. I found Melinda's body in the catacombs."

"I see." She nodded crisply, then mumbled some more, and finally hung up the phone. "He will speak with you after a positive identification of the body has been made. As of now, there is nothing he is able to discuss with you."

"But—" Sam managed to protest before she frowned and held up a flat palm to stop him.

She nodded once as if the matter were settled. "If you would leave your numbers, I will call you when he will try to make some time to speak with you."

Jess glanced at Sam from the corner of her eye and shook her head. She'd dealt with Parisian law enforcement before. She recognized a brick wall when she knocked her head against one.

She gave the woman both of their cell numbers and motioned Sam toward the door.

When they were out of hearing range, she said, "Crap."

"That's the best you can do?" Sam grinned. "Now what? Get your Paris office on the phone and use their influence to get us on the inside of the investigation?"

"Which would mean admitting I can't do this myself? No. At least, not yet." Jess said as they jogged down the steps. "Did you find out anything more about Trina and Melinda visiting the catacombs before the murder?"

Sam shook his head. "If you still have contact info for Trina, maybe we should start with a call to her and get the facts."

"Let's wait until they have a firm positive ID on the body before we drag Trina back into the situation. Besides, if Trina is guilty, tipping her off about Melinda's body in a phone call would be less effective than a personal interview."

Sam nodded. "Okay. So what do you want to do instead?"

"Check with the guide on the tourist desk at the catacombs. Find out if Trina and Melinda's names are listed in the guest logs. We can proceed from there, one way or the other."

"You think they have those logs on hand from two years ago?" Sam asked.

"Maybe." Jess shrugged and held her palm out flat. "Now you get in the passenger's seat and give me the keys. No offense, but you're an awful driver."

In a matter of minutes, they'd completed the short drive, parked the car, and stood at the tourist desk staring down at another French woman. This one was chubbier and more bored-looking than the last.

"Hello." Jess delivered another *Taboo* business card and smiled. "I'm wondering if you can help me?"

The woman nodded dubiously. From her expression, Sam figured she didn't understand a word of English.

"We are looking for a young woman who might have taken one of your tours a couple of years ago. Can you check and see if you have a record of Melinda McAllister?" Jess pointed to the computer and said the name slowly.

The woman stared at her blankly. Jess reached over the desk and grabbed a piece of note paper and a pen. She printed the name and handed it to the other woman. Jess pointed at the computer again.

This time, the message seemed to click. The woman stared at her screen and tapped away at her keyboard. She looked at Jess and shook her head. "No. I...erm...she is not here." She pointed at the screen. "You would like me to call my...erm...*Patron*?"

Sam focused, trying to untwist her accent, and when he finally understood her, he spoke up. "Your boss? You can ask your boss?"

She nodded, her plain face lighting up at the moment of successful communication.

"That would be great. We'd really appreciate it." He nodded, gave her a thumb's up and a big smile.

She smiled and nodded in return. "He is lunch right now. One hour?"

"Perfect." Sam nodded. He plucked the paper up, and he added his cell number for her. A few more smiles, nods, and he

FATAL ACTION | 123

was able to break away. He took a few paces and lowered his head close to Jess. "So what do we do for the next hour?"

"The tours are open," Jess looked toward a sign hanging above the desk.

"We can walk through on our own."

Jess frowned. "I'd rather see where you found the body without a tour guide watching us, too."

"Two options. These tunnels snake through the whole of the city, but they're off limits. It's illegal to explore them without a licensed tour guide. We can go to the street near where the body was found and look for an entrance. If we get caught, it's slap on the wrist and a hundred-dollar fine. I'm told people make a hobby of it here." He paused.

Jess raised her eyebrows.

"Or, if you'd rather avoid any possibility of arrest, we can go to one of the authorized sections and explore without a guide. But we won't be able to see the spot you're looking for."

"Can you locate the exact location without a map or a guide?"

Sam thought hard. "Near Rue du Rouge?"

"That's not far. We passed it on the way here." Jess had chewed her lower lip before she nodded decisively. "Let's get to work."

They power walked to the cobblestoned street. For the next thirty minutes, they scoured the buildings and alleys, searching for an entrance to the catacombs below. No luck.

"We might have to rethink," Sam said, wiping a thin sheen of perspiration from his upper lip.

"Keep a lookout." Jess jerked her head to the right. "One last look."

She stalked over to the corner of a bakery, squatted down,

and stretched her neck to peek into the little window beneath the building's front stoop.

"Well?" Sam asked, glancing back and forth to be sure no curious onlookers were watching.

"We're in luck."

He gaped. "Seriously?"

"This is an entrance." Without another word, Jess pulled the strap of her purse over her head and across her body. She opened the window and shimmied into the little space.

Sam glanced around again. No one seemed to notice the disappearance of a full-grown woman through the window. When her purse slipped through the dark hole behind her, Sam rushed under the stoop and stared into the darkness.

A moment later, Jess turned on the light of her phone. In the gleam, he saw her standing in a small puddle of water surrounded by smooth, graffitied stone walls.

"Come on, time's ticking," she said.

He looked around up top one last time, took a deep breath, and slid down to join her. He winced as his shoulders momentarily caught on the close walls of the space. He sucked in a calming breath through his nose and pushed through, letting out a relieved sigh when his feet hit the ground. Water splashed up from the stone floor and dampened his shoes.

"Look familiar?" Jess asked.

"No. And yes. All of these tunnels look the same. That's how people get lost down here." But then he heard something low and distant. Perhaps it was the sound of echoing feet and muffled voices.

He put a finger across his lips. "I think we're close. I can hear the tour."

He motioned for her to follow him. He moved toward the

noises. He whispered, "We're looking for a sort of carved-out section. That's where I found the body."

The tour group sounds were louder now, and a new light poured into the darkness from nearby. They were getting closer to the group. The light grew brighter. Jess moved to slide her phone into her pocket and in the jerk of her arm, he saw it.

"Wait, hold that out again, to the left. Your phone."

Jess did as he asked. They both saw it immediately—the metal door and the little alcove where he'd found Melinda McAllister's mutilated body. Except now the body had been removed and, in the same place, he saw a puddle of dark, reddish liquid.

"Is that blood?" Jess whispered.

Another noise sounded, and they turned. This wasn't the distant shuffling of feet or the droning of a tour guide, either. Someone was much closer.

Sam's adrenaline spiked. "Hello?"

No response.

CHAPTER FOUR

SAM GRAPPLED IN HIS back pocket for his phone and pulled it out. There were no signal bars in the corner of the screen.

He looked up at Jess just as another loud clanging sounded in the distance.

"Hello?" he called again. Still no response. The noises stopped abruptly, which increased his unease.

"Do you have cell service?" he asked as they both stepped toward the puddle, which looked like a mix of blood and water.

Jess glanced at her phone and shook her head. "We ought to call the police, though. There's no telling what's down here."

Or who.

The unspoken words hung in the air between them. He stared at her, knowing she was right. Unwilling to do what she asked.

Not that he didn't trust the *Police Nationale*. Just the opposite. They'd handled the initial situation professionally enough. But he'd been a cop for most of his life. He knew how things went. By the time the police arrived, the evidence could be gone and the perpetrator right along with it. Other lives were at risk, too. Sam would be the one directly responsible if he failed to act when he had the chance.

Gnawing the inside of his cheek, he fought back a stab of guilt he still suffered from all the times he'd failed to follow his gut. When he waited for the evidence and the warrants. Every time, more innocent people like Melinda McAllister paid the price.

It didn't matter what anyone said. Sam knew the truth. If he'd followed his gut, more often than not, he'd have saved the innocents whose haunted faces still plagued his nightmares. But he'd had a badge to lose and a job to keep. Now, he was a free agent. He wouldn't err on the side of caution. Not again.

"We're unarmed, Sam. I didn't have time to get the paperwork for my gun. We need firepower. Let's go back up and get the cops." Jess put her hand on his arm to get his attention.

Sam shook his head. "You go. I'm going to push forward. This red stuff is probably fresh blood. Somebody could be hurt."

"We don't know what's going on down there." She turned her phone to the winding tunnels around them. "We don't even know exactly where to look."

"It's a risk I'm willing to take. Someone is in trouble here. Don't you feel it?"

Jess blinked, then sucked in her bottom lip. She nodded. "Trouble is, I do."

"So I'm going in deeper. See what I can see."

"Okay. I'm not letting you go in there alone." Jess cocked her head for a moment then gave a curt nod. "But I'd feel a lot better if we were armed."

"Yeah. Me, too." Sam's grin was a little sickly. "How are you at hand-to-hand combat?"

"Not bad," she replied. "You?"

"Been a while since I had to find out." He shrugged and moved ahead. Jess followed.

They pushed forward, navigating the twists and turns, stopping every few yards to listen. They passed rows of stacked boulders until they came upon a pile of rocks that looked different from the rest. Oddly out of place. Some sort of shrine made of mounded, crumbling stones and topped with a skull.

Sam checked for fresh blood on the shrine, but saw none. He looked at Jess, and she shook her head. He made a mental note to mention the shrine to the police when they returned topside. His entire body hummed with the certainty that a much more urgent matter was ahead.

As he pushed forward, his cell phone flashlight caught a crack in the wall behind the odd shrine. Sam peered around the stones. The crack widened into a small tunnel back there. The shrine's placement was a marker to another part of the tunnels.

"I can crawl through that opening. It'll be tight." He turned to look at Jess, and she shook her head as another sound—this one almost like the rattle of chains—echoed from the space. He shook off the fanciful idea that there were malevolent ghosts behind the pile of stones.

"It's too low, Sam. You'll be crouched, closed in, with no way to protect yourself." She put a hand on his shoulder. "Let's go get the police."

Sam remembered all the times he'd waited and wished he hadn't.

"It probably opens up, farther along." He shook his head. "I'll keep moving. You go up and call them. Bring them back with you."

"Sam, it's not safe. You could—"

"Nothing you say is going to stop me, Jess. Make the call. Please."

Jess opened her mouth to argue again, but before she got the chance he ducked and crawled inside the small, dark opening.

He wriggled through the dirty, crumbling tunnel until he saw a dim light shining at the end. A whoosh of newfound anxiety passed through him. He crawled faster, careful to be as quiet as possible, focused on listening for sounds ahead.

He heard nothing more.

When he reached the end of the tunnel, the light fell on something new.

Half a second later, his brain caught up with what he saw.

The twisted, mangled body of a young man. Long dark hair covered his face save for his gaping, opened mouth. From his throat, dark blood had leaked to the ground, staining his shirt and jeans before it mixed with the water on the bottom of the tunnel.

Sam's breath caught. He scrambled backward, but it was too late.

A bright light shone into his eyes, temporarily blinding him.

A hand grabbed his hair and pulled him off his feet and heaved him into the pool of watered blood beside the bloody body.

"Why can't people leave us alone?" A deep angry voice said.

Sam squinted into the light, trying to make out the man's face. He was wearing a miner's hat with a spotlight on top. The light was so bright it pierced Sam's eyes and went straight to the pain centers in his brain.

The man was thin. Smaller than Sam. With the right leverage, Sam could overpower him.

"People ought to leave things as they are," the man growled, still angry.

The voice seemed oddly familiar. Sam tried to place it.

He tried to crab walk backward, away from his attacker. *Keep him talking.* "The police are on the way."

"I didn't want to kill you." He loomed closer.

Sam jumped to his feet. He lunged for the opening in the wall. But the man was faster.

A quicksilver flash. Sharp, biting pain exploded on Sam's right side. Warm blood began to flow down his torso.

Sam slapped his left palm over the gash. At the same time, his right hand shot up toward the light on the man's head and knocked the miner's hat askew.

Sam caught a quick glimpse of his face and a flash of red hair.

Shock rocketed through him, ramping his already pumping adrenaline higher.

He knew that face. Even with his features twisted into a mask of rage, Sam recognized the tour guide, Pierre.

Sam pressed his left hand to stabilize the knife in his side while his right arm shoved Pierre's head with all his might.

Pierre went crashing into the wall.

But that was all Sam could manage. He slumped back against the stone wall, breathing in shallow spurts.

Hot, wet blood gushed down his side, sticking his clothes to his body. His vision blackened around the edges, darkness closing fast.

Pierre rose to his feet.

"They deserved to die. This is not a playground." Pierre loomed closer. In the deflected light from the helmet, Sam saw his wild eyes...the hot spots of color on his pale cheeks.

Sam tried to stay calm, sure that his pounding heart would force blood to ooze faster from his body.

"Sam!"

Distant but distinct. He sucked in a breath and managed a grunt in return.

"Sam," Jess yelled again. "We're coming!"

Pierre glanced from Sam to the crawl space between them and the open passage to the tunnels. He paused. A frown collapsed his thick eyebrows. He snarled and swore and sprinted away in the opposite direction through another tunnel Sam hadn't noticed before.

Sam closed his eyes. The gooey mess between his fingers was warm and flowed with each heartbeat. The sounds of scuffling feet came closer.

A policeman paused at the entrance, crouched on all fours, gun drawn. "Are you alone?" he asked.

"He ran that way." Sam managed to point.

The officer scuttled through the small opening and stood as Jess appeared behind him. She gasped as she looked from the dead man to Sam.

"Medic!" she screamed.

"Madame, please. You need to go back," the police officer said as he squatted to the ground and felt the young man's carotid pulse. The action was purely reflex. The boy was long dead.

Sam pointed to the dark, meeting Jess's gaze as she dropped to her knees beside him. "He went that way. It was Pierre, my tour guide from the day we found Melinda."

A medic ducked into the opening from the crawl space.

Jess took Sam's hand and squeezed.

Her mouth was moving, but her words seemed slurred, and his vision flickered. When the medic tugged his hand away from the knife in his side, agony tore through him again.

Sam glanced at the body of the young man a few feet away once more as he slipped into oblivion.

Too little, too late...again.

CHAPTER FIVE

Four days later

SAM SAT ALONE AT the table and took a long sip from his cup, savoring the aroma and the taste of the exquisite French press coffee. He would miss his new morning ritual. Watching people in the morning at his favorite patisserie as he tucked away a couple of croissants.

He took a hearty bite of his flaky, still-warm pastry.

"You know how much butter is in those?"

He looked up to see Jess Kimball coming his way. She walked with purpose like she had somewhere to be. He used to walk like that. Before he retired.

"Glad you're up and around again, Sam. But you keep eating those, you're going to drop dead of a heart attack before you hit sixty." She hefted her shoulder bag onto the tiny cafe table and sat.

"I figure I've used around six of my nine lives. That leaves me three more. I can sacrifice one for these little clouds of heaven. Besides, the doc released me."

"That so?"

He nodded. "I've got a recheck in a couple of weeks, but otherwise, nothing but a bit of soreness and an ugly scar to impress the women I date. I'm good."

He took another bite and grinned as the flaky pastry practically melted in his mouth. It seemed like they tasted even better today. From experience, he knew the sharpened pleasure would fade once the almost giddy high of being alive disappeared.

That feeling, the one that made the sky seem almost painfully blue, relishing the sun on his face, inhaling the subtle scent of cherry blossoms in the air, was far too fleeting. If someone could bottle the sheer intoxication of being alive after a near miss like he'd suffered, they'd make a mint.

Soon enough, he'd notice the clouds on the horizon, remember that the sun causes skin cancer, and curse his allergy to flowers of all kinds.

Such was life. For now, he'd revel in the euphoria as long as it lasted. And he'd keep being grateful that the knife Pierre stabbed him with had missed all his vital organs and wasn't contaminated with some deadly disease.

"Seriously, Sam, you were lucky. Don't take that luck for granted. You're not bulletproof, you know." Jess tugged a thick file folder from her bag and placed it on the table between them. "I spoke to the Inspector this morning. Seems like it's all locked up. The guy gave a full confession."

The waiter came and took Jess's order. Sam grinned when she ordered a basket of croissants and her own pot of French Press coffee with cream.

"When in France," she said with a wink, before opening the file folder and handing him a sheaf of papers. "So get this. Your tour guide, Pierre? Turns out he's not your average homicidal maniac. He's a cataphile."

"I'm hoping that isn't what it sounds like." Sam frowned and scanned the documents in his hand absently. It was a copy of the police report, but it was all in French. "He, uh, likes sex with *cats*?"

She let out a short laugh and shook her head. "No. Cataphile refers to a whole group of urban explorers. They delve into the mines of Paris tunnels, including the catacombs. Even the ones that are technically off limits. They're a passionate bunch. They've got a set of unwritten rules about revering the tunnels. Some of them, like Pierre, are more than a little obsessive about it, as you noticed during the tour you took. Apparently, Melinda broke one of their rules when she went on the tour. She wanted to leave her mark on Paris, so she tagged one of the walls with her first name."

Sam shook his head, handing the papers back to Jess. "He killed her because she spray-painted her name on an old stone wall?"

He wasn't a fan of littering or of people who treated historical artifacts with disrespect, but Melinda was little more than a kid. It was a prank. Nothing she deserved to die for.

A chill washed over him. "Did he catch her in the act?"

They paused as the waiter came to deliver Jess's breakfast.

"That's the thing. He didn't see her. He wasn't working that day or the next. But Melinda was unlucky. Pierre was exploring the catacombs, though, which I guess he did daily. He saw the tag. He was outraged and removed it immediately." She paused as she pawed through her pastries and chose one. "When he went back to work, he typed her first name from the tag, into the computer. She was registered as a visitor. He tracked her down."

Sam chewed and swallowed slowly. "So the murder was premeditated."

Jess nodded and took a sip of her coffee. "He hunted her. Followed her to class. Took note of her habits for a full week. Then he orchestrated a meeting at her favorite bar the night she went missing."

"What about Trina? Why didn't he kill her, too?"

"She wasn't at the bar that night. Trina was still angry after their big fight a couple of days earlier. And Trina didn't deface the walls of the catacombs, either. Fortunately for her. But once the police identified Trina as a suspect, the press picked it up," she shrugged. "The rest is history."

"I guess his stealthy planning and unusual motivation helped keep him under the radar, too." Sam nodded. "He was damn lucky. Melinda and Trina were not so lucky."

"Things sometimes work out that way, Sam." Jess placed a hand on his forearm. "But Trina's grateful to you for solving the case now."

"Yeah," he grimaced. "Just once, I'd like to get there before the bad guys do the deed, you know?"

"I know. But this time, for Trina, it was truly better late than never."

"I suppose." Sam picked up the file again and sifted through until he came across the photo. A young, vibrant Melinda stared back at him, a smile full of mischief. "Damn shame. And the young man I found? Same thing?"

"He and a couple of friends brought some weed and beer for a party. Pierre followed them. He planned to lure them into that opening, one at a time." Jess leaned in and gave him a sad smile. "We weren't able to save Melinda or that young man, but we did some good here, Sam. Your finding Melinda and taking action likely saved more lives. We know how this goes. Once a man like Pierre starts killing, he doesn't stop."

Sam put the photo down with a sigh. The faces would stay with him forever, but Jess was right. Stopping Pierre from killing again had to be enough. "So now what?"

Jess tucked a lock of curly blonde hair behind one ear. "You mean since he confessed can he still get off on some sort of technicality? I don't know what the law is here in France, so it's hard to say. Since there is no death penalty here, I doubt he'll try. He's proud of his handiwork. My guess is that it's over."

"You must be relieved. You were right. Trina was innocent after all. Maybe she can finally get her life back on track."

"What life she has left. This has been ruinous for her. She's lived under a cloud for more than two years. Lost her friends. Had to drop out of school because she couldn't deal with the harassment. Couldn't get a job." Jess frowned as she picked off a piece of her croissant. "But she's a strong young woman. I hope she'll be able to turn things around."

"Better than if Melinda's body had never been found, at least." He needed this. Just a narrow silver lining he could cling to.

"True. And Melinda's family can finally lay her to rest. So what's next for you?" Jess restacked the papers and took one last look at the photo. She slipped everything into the folder. "You said you were going to start a security firm in Denver? When is that launching?"

That was the question, wasn't it? But now, the photo of Melinda's smiling face still etched in his mind, he shrugged. "I planned to start my own agency. Now? I don't know, Jess. Personal security might be okay. I feel like I could make a solid living, get my second kid the rest of the way through college, and then put together a nice little nest egg."

"But?" she urged, a smile tugging at her lips.

"But there wouldn't be this, you know? As bad as it gets, there's no replacement for feeling like you've helped somebody."

What he'd done here certainly felt better than walking a paranoid businessman through a crowded airport or watching over a touring starlet while she signed autographs at the local concert venue.

"Whether it's saving a life, or getting a violent criminal off the street, or giving a parent some closure…all that stuff feels more important to me today than I realized when I left Denver P.D." He grimaced when he realized what he'd said and felt a guilty stab to his heart.

He hadn't asked her about her son. But what was there to say? He knew Peter was still missing and he had nothing positive to offer her. He looked down at the table and let the urge to mention painful subjects pass.

"You're a good guy, Sam. Denver P.D. should welcome your return in a heartbeat." Her voice was strong and her smile genuine. Whatever her private pain, she had pushed it aside for the moment. "If they won't take you back, let me know. I think I could help you find something."

He smiled his thanks and then swallowed down the last of his coffee. "I appreciate that. If I can be of any help to you, anything at all, call me, and I'll be ready." He stood and tossed some bills on the table between them. Her eyes were glassy, and the last thing he wanted was to steal what little joy she'd found. "I've got to head out. There's a tour of the Louvre starting in fifteen."

She raised her cup. "I'm going to hang back and enjoy my coffee and the calm for a few minutes. My flight leaves in a couple hours and then it's back to the grind."

He nodded one last time and shuffled off toward the museum. She called after him.

"Hey, Sam?"

He turned and shot her a questioning glance.

"Do me a favor and just stick to the tour, okay? No veering off. I think I've used up all my goodwill with the *Police Nationale* for a while. If they see us coming, they might decide to lock us up."

He gave her a grin and a thumb's up then kept walking.

THE END

FATAL
HEAT

CAST OF PRIMARY CHARACTERS

Jessica Kimball
Marilyn Pleva

CHAPTER ONE

JESS KIMBALL'S FRIEND, SHERIFF Marilyn Pleva, rounded the corner of the terracotta truck stop building, covering her mouth and nose as she peered behind the dumpster.

It had been more than two years since she'd smelled it, but there was no mistaking the stench. Hundred-degree heat and a dead body produced a predictable result, no matter *how* dry that heat was. This New Mexico summer was nothing if not hot.

Already, the flies were swarming, and the incessant buzzing made the hair on her arms stand up.

She steeled herself and, scanning the ground to avoid disturbing the evidence, moved closer to the lifeless form a few yards away.

When the nine-one-one call came in ten minutes ago, the dispatcher said the caller reported a child victim. Marilyn hoped the trucker had made a mistake.

He hadn't.

She pinched her eyes closed and muttered a string of curses, ending on a prayer.

One of Santo Christo's own. A petite girl, smaller than average for her age.

Owen and Alicia Cabbot's daughter, Emily.

The couple owned Sinful Sweets bakery, located about a mile down the road from where Emily's body had been dumped right next to the trash.

"Jesus, God," a low voice muttered from just behind her.

She turned to find one of her deputies, Brady Colton, standing there, gun extended, his face chalky with shock. For a second, she wondered if he might be sick, but he rallied. She edged closer to Emily as Brady circled the immediate area in case whoever dumped her here was still in the vicinity.

"All clear," he said, reappearing from behind the dumpster.

"Go ahead and call the ME. Tell them to get here ASAP before the hot sun makes things even worse," Marilyn said, squatting down low to examine the body as the deputy made the call.

She would wait for the ruling from the Office of the Medical Examiner, but forced to guess the cause of death, it looked like a broken neck. Probably pretty close to instant.

Marilyn saw no signs of any harm that might have been inflicted before death. She had not been sexually assaulted or otherwise harmed.

"Animals," Brady muttered, his eyes bloodshot with unshed tears. "Who could do this to a kid? I don't understand it."

She shook her head. "Let's not jump to conclusions before we have more facts."

Privately, she recognized her cautionary words for what they were. Denial. Plain and simple. In fact, her inability to accept the violence people were capable of was what had caused her to move to a small town. She'd seen too many bodies. She'd wanted to return to helping people, not solving murders.

For two years, she'd had a break. Sure, a few drunk and disorderlies escalated into domestic violence now and then. The fight over at the Twisted Tavern that went too far had the whole town reeling last Christmas.

But children murdered? Not what she'd fled here for. The bastard who did this wouldn't be walking around free for long. Which would be precious little comfort to Emily or her family, even though it was the best Marilyn could possibly do now.

She resisted the urge to sweep a lock of long, blond hair away from the girl's heatbloated face and straightened.

"Tape it off, all the way back the scrub brush. You stay here while I go inside, let them know they're closed for business, and ask some questions."

"Roger that," Brady replied, heading back the way he'd come to retrieve the tape from his trunk.

Marilyn glanced at her watch, swiping a hand over her already sweat-dotted upper lip. Six-thirty a.m. There had been no missing persons reports recently. Which meant that Owen and Alicia Cabbot likely had no idea that their daughter was missing, let alone dead.

The city cop in her couldn't help adding a mental caveat. *Unless of course, the parents were the ones responsible.*

She let her eyes drift closed as she called up a mental image of the couple.

Alicia was blond like her daughter, with deep blue eyes and a sweet disposition. She perpetually smelled of cinnamon and baking bread. All of which made her easy to like, although she wasn't much of a talker.

Her husband was the more social of the two, quick to laugh and always up for a beer and chat session after a long day of manning the counter. Marilyn knew Owen better, and while she wouldn't have categorized him as the town drunk, he certainly enjoyed his beer.

In the time she'd lived in Santo Christo, she recalled dealing with him officially a couple times. Once, when she'd pulled him over for a DUI. About six months later, he'd accepted her offer of a ride home after a particularly boisterous football game at the local sports bar left him too drunk to drive.

Neither occasion provoked Owen to any kind of violence. He was a happy drunk.

As far as Marilyn knew, the Sheriff's Office had never received any domestic calls for the Cabbot household, either. Whenever she saw thirteen-year-old Emily and her younger brother Billy, they'd always seemed healthy and typical of kids in town. Emily loved helping out at the bakery. She'd rung up Marilyn's morning coffee and almond scone more than once.

Now, she had to go to that quaint little house on Elderberry Lane and tell those parents the worst news any parents could ever receive.

Who in their right mind would sign up for this job?

"Pippa is on her way over and Santa Fe OMI is twenty minutes out," Brady said as he approached with a roll of yellow tape. Pippa Reynolds was a sharp new deputy and Marilyn was relieved for the extra set of hands.

She headed around to the front to the truck-stop building's entrance. As she stepped inside, the air-conditioned room's chill enveloped her. Normally, like every New Mexicano in July, she welcomed the cold. This morning, though, she felt iced to the bone.

"Sheriff? Was it…" The clerk's Adam's apple bobbed up and down in his skinny neck as he swallowed audibly. "Was it what that trucker said?"

She tipped her head in a grim nod and leaned across the counter to take the teenager gently by the arm. "I'm so sorry to say it was, Nate."

His top lip caught on his braces as his mouth trembled. Poor kid had graduated high school a few weeks ago and switched to the overnight shift. Probably never thought he'd experience something like this.

"What if she was alive out there? Could I have helped her?" The tremor traveled from his face down to the hand she was holding.

Marilyn shook her head. "Nothing you could've done. You had no way of knowing. The best way to help her now is to find out what happened here. Walk me through your shift last night."

Having a task seemed to calm him some. She took out her notebook as he began to talk. She jotted down the names of the late-night customers that he recognized and descriptions of ones he didn't. The whole time, though, one thought played in her mind over and over again as dread formed an oil slick in her belly.

In just a short while, she would ring Alicia Cabbot's doorbell, look into her soft, blue eyes, and tell her that her daughter was never coming home.

CHAPTER TWO

AN HOUR LATER, MARILYN squeezed the steering wheel, staring at the small, white house. It looked like it had originally been a ranch, converted to a bungalow by a small airport room on the roof. Probably two bedrooms and maybe two baths.

"Dammit," she mumbled. This was the whole reason she'd quit the city—to avoid visits like these...and the nightmares that haunted her long afterward.

Her stomach was trying to churn the knot in her gut, grinding it down until it was nothing but bile.

Marilyn huffed out a long breath and forced herself from the hot, black unmarked car. Not for the first time, she cursed the city council for buying the last of the Ford dealer's sedan inventory a couple of years ago. The cars were dumped cheap because nobody in her right mind would want a black car with black interior during New Mexico's summers. She constantly felt twenty-six hours in on her twenty-four-hour deodorant.

Training her gaze on the cheery, bright red door of the Cabbot house, she inhaled deeply, chewed on the inside of her cheek, and knocked once.

She heard scuffling, low chatter, and the distant drone of the morning news network, which amplified as the door swung open. A bleary-eyed blonde in a floral bathrobe stood inside. The smell of coffee and a rush of cool air wafted out into the sweltering morning.

Before Marilyn could say anything, Owen moseyed up behind his wife. His slippered feet gently shushed as they slid along the hardwood floor.

"Alicia…" Marilyn started, but the young mom cut her off, sleepy eyes widening.

"Hey, Marilyn, what's going on? Everything okay?" She glanced from Marilyn to her husband, as if trying to read the answer in their faces. "Why are you here?"

Marilyn could almost see the gears grinding in Alicia's mind as she searched to find an explanation for the sheriff's early morning visit that wouldn't obliterate her life.

No way past it but straight through.

Marilyn cleared her aching throat.

"I'm sorry to tell you that, earlier this morning, I was called to a crime scene," Marilyn the official words in a practiced professional tone. The best thing was to just say them quickly. "Alicia…Owen…we believe the victim found at the scene was your daughter, Emily. I'm so very sorry for your loss."

Alicia's nostrils flared. She blinked as if she didn't comprehend. It was a sickening, taut moment that stretched out for an eternity. Marilyn felt every millisecond.

Owen gripped his wife's shoulders from behind as she shook her head furiously, his face going slack.

"No. No, no, no. That's not possible." At first, Alicia's voice was little more than a whisper. But then, she was almost shouting. "Th-the kids are sleeping. This is a mistake. We—"

She stopped mid-sentence, tearing away from her husband's grasp and pounded through the house, the tail of her robe flying behind her.

She muttered about the kids still being in bed—about how they were sleeping in longer than usual today.

Alicia raced up the steep stairs to the airport room, opened the door at the top, and crumpled against the doorframe. Marilyn climbed the stairs heavily. She already knew what she'd see when she peered in.

Or, at least she thought she knew.

But when the sight of a stacked pair of twin beds—both mussed from sleep, both empty—greeted her, she sucked in a breath. The floor was littered with toys and books. She searched frantically for the eight-year-old boy who should've been sleeping in the bottom bunk.

She saw no blood.

No broken glass.

And no Billy.

Alicia's low, keening wail cut through the silence. Owen's face, so white it was nearly gray, grasped her shoulders, pulling her close against his chest.

Adrenaline shot through Marilyn like an electric charge. She grabbed her radio and stepped away. She called the station and reported Billy Cabbot, officially a missing child.

She ordered an immediate Amber Alert.

She told the dispatcher to send a dog and handler along with a small search team to scour the area around the truck stop.

"The Amber Alert for Billy is already out," she said when she returned to the bewildered parents. Her phone chimed in her back pocket as if to underscore the words, but the Cabbots didn't seem to hear.

Owen held his wife close, both arms wrapped around her, solemn.

Too solemn?

Marilyn wanted to comfort them. But she had to focus. Find Billy.

"I cannot imagine your suffering, and I'm so sorry. I truly am. I know this must be the worst day of your lives, but—" She had to press them now. It was barbaric. But every passing minute was a missed opportunity for Billy. "We need to get Billy home safe, all right? I need to ask some questions."

Alicia pushed her face away from her husband's chest. Her gaze shot to Marilyn. She nodded blankly, swiping a hand over her wet nose and mouth.

"Okay. Yes." She turned to her husband, probably in shock. "Right Owen? We need to get Billy home."

Alicia pinned her watery gaze on Marilyn. "What do you need?"

"Let's get some coffee, and figure out our next steps. We need to move very quickly." ...*If it's not already too late for Billy.*

The unspoken words hung in the air. Alicia nodded slowly, allowing Owen to guide her toward the kitchen.

Alicia sat at one of the high-backed stools in front of the granite countertop, and while Owen made coffee, Marilyn considered the options. If statistics held true, they had about forty-eight hours. After that, the chances of finding Billy alive diminished by the minute.

Think like the killer. Who is he? Where is he? What's really going on here?

But what kind of person would take both kids, kill the girl, and leave the boy alive?

Assuming Billy was still alive.

Marilyn pushed the thought aside. She refused to consider the alternative.

Her best guess, informed by years of investigating child homicide, made the situation worse.

If Emily's killer was a pedophile who preyed on boys, why take Emily at all?

Owen slid a mug in front of Marilyn, still silent as the grave, and took a seat beside his wife.

Alicia was shaking, letting out little gasps and hiccups as she choked back her tears. But there was a thin wall of strength holding her together. Like the skin beneath the shell of an egg, one false move and she might shatter.

Marilyn's job was to walk both parents through the interview and get as much information as she could before that happened.

She pulled out her notepad. "Tell me about last night and the last time you saw Emily."

Alicia turned watery eyes on her husband and he cleared his throat.

"It was our anniversary." His voice was coarse and rusty, like he'd broken a long vow of silence. "The day was normal. The kids went to school and came home. We went to work and came home. At about six o'clock, our friend, Tim Wagoner, came over to watch the kids for the evening so Alicia and I could go out and celebrate, just the two of us."

Marilyn had seen Wagoner around town a few times, but couldn't recall having spoken to him more than once or twice. She scribbled down the name.

Alicia piped in nervously. "He's a good friend of ours. He really helped us when we were first getting settled in town. We've known him for years."

Marilyn nodded, careful not to say that stranger danger was a myth. Far more often, the people you knew, the ones you least expected, committed these crimes.

It was too early for theories, though. She encouraged the Cabbots to continue.

"We went to Vincenzo's and had dinner. We'd had a little to drink. A bottle of wine," Alicia said, heat rushing to her face.

"Maybe two," Owen added. A devastated expression settled over his heavy brow.

"But when we got home, the children were in bed asleep. There was nothing unusual about it. We thanked Tim, kissed the kids good night, and went to sleep ourselves." Alicia shook her head, clearly in distress. "Oh my God, how did we not hear someone in the house stealing them right from under our noses?" Her husband's face settled into a mask of regret.

If Owen was admitting to two bottles of wine, he could very well have swallowed more. They might have passed out and slept through the kidnapping. Possibly.

Marilyn pursed her lips. A firm knock sounded at the front door. "That's probably the crime scene investigation team. They're here to take a look at the kids' room. Please excuse me for a moment?"

Both Cabbots nodded as Marilyn made for the door. She noticed a man's hat on the side table and gestured to it. "Whose is that?"

"Pastor Tim's," Owen said. "He wears it all the time. He must've forgotten it last night when he left."

She nodded and turned her attention back to opening the door. The head investigator, a stern-looking woman named Mirabel Vasquez, gave her a stiff nod. Marilyn moved aside as Vasquez and her male assistant walked in, laden with equipment.

"The room is on the second floor, at the top of the stairs."
She ushered them in the right direction.

Marilyn's deputies, Pippa and Brady, trailed behind. "You
two, walk the perimeter of the house. Tag anything that seems
even remotely unusual."

Marilyn bustled out the front door and made her way to the
sauna that was her car. The emotion inside the house blanketed
everything like the stifling air, weighing her down.

Sliding into the driver's seat, she started the engine and
turned the air conditioning up full blast. Sweat beaded on her
forehead as she located her personal phone and dialed Jess
Kimball's number.

Marilyn knew the famous journalist well. They'd worked
together before.

Jess kept a sharp eye on child kidnappings. For years, she'd
been traveling the country working tirelessly on behalf of crime
victims, hoping to find her own son, who'd been taken when he
was barely a toddler. Jess was an expert and she'd be more than
willing to help if she could.

The line clicked to life and then Jess's voice came through,
"Hey there, stranger.

What's going on?"

"Unfortunately, nothing good." Marilyn opted to rip off the
bad news fast. "We found a girl dead this morning. I just left the
parents. It appears that their young son is also missing."

Jess's silence filled the connection. Marilyn gave her a
chance to absorb the news. Every time Jess heard a story like
this, it had to eat away at her soul, but that level of empathy and
commitment was what made her such a bulldog.

"Okay, lay it on me," Jess said, her tone clipped and all
business.

Marilyn relayed the particulars of the body, and the information she'd gathered from the Cabbots. "Any chance you could head down here and help out?"

"I wish I could, but I'm on another case at the moment." Jess paused. "I'll make some calls. See if there's been anything similar reported. As you get more details, please—"

"I'll let you know."

"My one piece of advice here, Marilyn? I feel sorry for anyone who suffers this as a parent. Believe me, I know how that is. It's worse because you know these parents, and the kids. But everyone is a suspect. The odds are…" Jess trailed off because Marilyn didn't need her to finish.

Whoever took the children more than likely knew them. Well enough that neither of the Cabbot kids had put up much of a fight. They'd most likely walked out of that house, thinking everything was just fine.

And now at least one of them was never coming back.

Marilyn swore and stuffed her cell phone back into her pocket.

CHAPTER THREE

IT WAS BARELY NINE o'clock and the summer sun beat down on her car forcing the air conditioning to work overtime with very little success. Droplets of sweat pooled along her brow and dripped down the back of her neck.

Forty-eight hours.

She imagined she heard the ticking clock.

Somehow, even with her small crew, she had to interview the Cabbots, all their friends and family, everyone who could possibly know or have seen the kids—school, teachers, day care, bakery employees, truckers at the truck stop, too.

She was exhausted just thinking about it. But first, she'd go inside and get the preliminary information from the crime scene techs.

She stepped from the stifling hot car into the marginally cooler morning, and covered the winding path to the door quickly. The doorknob scorched her palm as she turned it.

Wincing, she looked up to find the lead crime tech staring.

"Jane," Marilyn said, "What do you have for me?"

The older woman shook her head. "Not much of anything in

the bedroom. Nothing broken, the window was still locked. Luminol did turn up some trace blood on the girl's pillowcase, though."

"Probably from a nosebleed." Alicia had appeared at Jane's shoulder. She must have overheard the conversation from her seat in the kitchen. "She always gets…" She stopped short, closed her eyes, took a deep breath, and then corrected herself, "she *used* to get nosebleeds in the middle of the night during summertime. The doctor said it was because of the dry heat."

Jane nodded. "That would be consistent with what we found. It was deep in the fibers of the pillow case, which was covered by the blankets, and nowhere else. We're pulling prints. We need prints from the parents to exclude them."

Marilyn looked to Alicia, who nodded, "Of course."

"Sounds good. Give me five more minutes and they're all yours." Jane tipped her head in a clipped nod and stalked off.

Marilyn guided Alicia toward the kitchen. Alicia settled onto a stool while Marilyn pulled out her notepad. It still only had one name written in Marilyn's precise hand—Tim Wagoner, and then later, she'd added, Pastor. Before the day was over, there'd likely be two dozen or so names on the list.

"Okay, we've found no obvious signs of a struggle. So far, we have no point of forced entry. Do you lock your doors every night?"

"Yes, but," Alicia looked at her husband, "I don't recall if we did last night."

"I locked up same as always, right after Tim left."

"Do you leave a spare key somewhere? Inside or outside the house?" Marilyn asked.

Alicia shook her head. "I saw on television that you weren't supposed to."

"And does anyone else have the keys to your house other than the two of you?" Marilyn asked, a little more firmly this time. "Really think. Anyone who watched the place during a vacation, maybe?"

"No, nobody—" Owen started, but he was interrupted by the smack of a window opening and colliding with the sill. Brady had been studying the window panes along the kitchen wall, and he blinked in surprise before turning to face Marilyn.

"This one was unlocked," Brady said. "Slid right open."

"But I…" Alicia looked from her husband to Marilyn and back again. "I always keep the windows locked. I don't…"

"What about last weekend? When you were heavy cleaning? Didn't you pop the windows out and wash them?" Owen prompted.

"I did," Alicia said with a nod. "I locked them all back up. But maybe I missed one. It's possible. Oh my God, please don't tell me. Are my children gone because of me?" She shuddered and slumped forward.

Marilyn turned her attention back on Owen. "Is there anyone I can call? Someone who can come and support you both?"

"My mother," Alicia sniffed. "Her number…" She pointed to the fridge.

On the gleaming surface of the fridge was a sticky note with the words "Emergency Contacts" written in red, curly letters.

"The pastor's number is on there, too. Call him here to pray with us," Owen added, then focused on rubbing his wife's back.

Marilyn moved over to the fridge, reviewing the names. She snapped a photo of the list with her cell phone before she called Alicia's mother.

It was, she supposed, a small service to break the news of Emily's death for the Cabbots, to save them from saying the words themselves just yet.

The pastor and Alicia's mother arrived in record time. No more than fifteen minutes had elapsed. They joined Alicia and Owen in the living room.

The foursome held hands, heads bowed, as the TV droned quietly in the background.

"Dear Lord," Pastor Wagoner's voice quavered, and his face was pale, but he pressed on, glancing from Alicia to Owen as he prayed.

The prayer went on for a long moment. When it was over, Marilyn stepped in and pulled Owen aside.

"It's a formality. And I'm sorry. But we're going to need you down to the Medical Examiner's office to identify the body as soon as they're ready."

She watched his expression carefully as she spoke. He remained impassive, nodding as he wiped away the one tear he'd shed as he prayed. "Is there anything else I can do for you?"

"I need to talk to the pastor about his time with the kids last night."

Owen nodded, then crossed the room to tap Pastor Wagoner on the arm. He whispered to Wagoner, who shot her a glance and nodded. Marilyn flipped to a fresh page in her notebook.

Okay, Pastor Tim Wagoner, last to see the Cabbot children both awake and alive.

Let's see what you know about all this.

Marilyn guided Wagoner outside. The crime techs needed more space. And she didn't want the family to overhear.

The sun was higher in the sky now and it hammered down in a nearly tangible way.

She ushered him under the little, shaded stoop.

"Sorry to drag you out in the heat. Hopefully we won't be too long," she said.

"Anything I can do to help."

"You've known the family for a while?"

"Probably four, five years, something like that. Helped them rustle up some business for their bakery." He shook his head and closed his eyes briefly. "They're good people.

Emily and Billy are good kids. Such a tragedy."

"Tell me what happened last night, as specifically as you can."

"Not much to tell. Alicia and Owen were celebrating their wedding anniversary. They needed a sitter. I volunteered."

"Did you have a close relationship with the children?"

"I'm not sure what you're implying. Same as the other families who invite me to their homes." His brow wrinkled into a deep frown. "I mean, Marilyn, I don't have to tell you—this is a small town. We all know each other."

She nodded and made a note. "Were the kids acting unusually in any way last night?"

He considered that and shook his head. "Not that I noticed. Emily was excited because she won the coin flip to pick a movie. I warmed up the dinner Alicia left for us. When the movie ended, we frosted some cookies Alicia made earlier. After that, Emily read a chapter of one of those books Billy likes. We said our prayers and they went up to bed."

"And what did you do after they went to sleep?"

"I watched SportsCenter," he said with a half-smile. "Even men of God like sports, you know."

Marilyn feigned a grin. "I meant after the Cabbots returned home. What did you do next?"

Brown caterpillar eyebrows pulled tight and his thin face grew heavy with creases.

"Am I under suspicion, Sheriff?"

"Nobody is accusing you of anything, Tim," she answered carefully. "I need to get a solid timeline, to rule out as many people as I can. So we're free to focus on the people who can't account for themselves."

He watched her a moment before he cocked his head. "Well, I said good night to the Cabbots. I went to the gas station near my house where I filled up my car and picked up a bottle of water. I think I still have the receipt in my wallet. The church reimburses me for car expenses. Which is a good thing, given how much gas that big, black monster guzzles."

Marilyn waited.

He rustled in his back pocket and pulled out a worn brown leather billfold. He let it fall open and grabbed a wrinkled paper sticking out from the top.

After a cursory glance at the slip, he handed it over. "Looks like it was eleven thirtysix last night."

Marilyn took the receipt. "And after that?"

He shrugged. "I went home and hit the hay."

"I do have an awfully nosy neighbor, Mrs. Willis. She can likely tell you whether she saw my car in the driveway." He paused and when she didn't dismiss the matter out of hand, challenged, "Would you like her number?"

"For formality's sake, if you don't mind."

"Not at all. We depend on our police." He rattled off the name and phone number.

"Thank you." Marilyn wiped a drop of sweat from her brow, glancing down at her notebook, as if she was searching for questions. "One last thing. Mr. and Mrs. Cabbot.

Are they—"

"They are impeccable. Mind you, Owen does have his demons, but he and Alicia are truly fine people and wonderful

parents." He pursed his lips into a grim line and glared at her.
"They would no more hurt those kids than, well, rob a bank or
something. If that's what you're thinking, just get that out of
your head right now."

Marilyn kept her face impassive. "Thank you so much for
your time."

"You have my number should you think of anything else,"
he said gruffly, as if he'd been sorely offended and wouldn't
soon forget her impertinence. She followed him into the house
and rounded up her deputies.

Pippa spoke first. "I compiled a list."

"Good," Marilyn said. "Let's go outside."

After they shared notes and divided the names, Marilyn
returned to her black car oven and read over Pippa's list. The
first name was a familiar one—James Valetti, the middle school
science teacher. Pippa thought it odd that Valetti spent quite a bit
of after school time with Billy. No school today, Saturday, but
Pippa had located his home address.

In a few short minutes, Marilyn pulled up in front of the
squat, yellow bungalow across town. Valetti was out front
washing his car, a sleek, black Jaguar. She wondered briefly how
he'd paid for it on a local teacher's salary.

When Marilyn stepped from her unmarked sedan, he froze.
Of course, he was familiar with local law enforcement vehicles.
Everyone in town recognized them on sight.

Valetti's response raised her internal radar.

"Morning, Sheriff." His short brown hair was mussed, and
he wore a dirty, greenstriped T-shirt long enough to cover the
indecent shorts that barely covered his ass.

"James, do you have a moment?"

He nodded and set down his soapy sponge. She broke the

news to him, watching his reaction with a practiced eye. His face blanched when she said Emily was dead and Billy was missing.

"Those poor people." He shook his head and blinked a few times. "How terrible." "Yes," Marilyn agreed.

"What do you need from me?" He asked, abruptly, swiping his eyes with the back of one hand.

Her gut said something about his reaction was off. "Well, as I understand it, you were close with Billy. Is that right?"

"He was—is—certainly a bright child. He stays after class on Wednesdays for extra science tutoring—he's a natural."

"I see." She nodded. "Has Billy, or Emily for that matter, been acting strangely or nervous or anything at all in school?"

"I can't say that they did." Valetti rolled his thumb over his bottom lip. "They're pretty quiet kids, though. Well behaved. Better than a lot of the pampered little monsters, you know?"

"I see." That the two kids were well adjusted was something everyone apparently agreed upon.

Still, his sudden tense shift when he was referring to Billy made her uneasy. "Do you assist other gifted students after school hours? Or just Billy?"

His face blanked. "Not regularly. Billy entered a rocket exhibit. He wanted to win the contest. I was—am—helping him with his model, which was darn good, by the way. He might actually take first place."

A boney knee shook and his hands fidgeted. His gaze darted to her hulking black car again.

Something wasn't right here. She couldn't put her finger on it, but the man was acting squirrely, setting her internal radar abuzz. "We need to account for everyone between the hours of eleven last night and five this morning. Where were you during that time, James?"

"Oh, I was at home," he answered quickly. "I mean, here."

If the quiver in his voice had anything to do with Emily and Billy, she might take him out right here. "Anyone who can confirm?"

"I was with a friend, yeah," he added, frantic now. "And your friend's name?" "CJ." He all but whispered.

"Just give me CJ's full name, address, and phone number, I'll be able to—"

"I can't." He cut her off. "I mean, I can, but it wouldn't be much help. CJ's on a flight to Mexico. Hopped on this morning. Totally incommunicado."

"Is that so?" She hardened her tone. "I'll take his name and number in any case."

"Uh, sure. Okay." He rattled off the information so quietly she had to lean closer to hear.

She jotted everything down and closed her notebook with a snap. "Thank you for your time. I'll be in touch."

"Right, okay, Sheriff." Valetti coughed, seemed about to say something, but he only nodded. "Let me know if there's anything else I can do."

She returned to her hot black oven and fished out her list of interview subjects while Valetti stared at her from the driveway.

CHAPTER FOUR

EIGHT HOURS LATER, MARILYN rubbed her tired eyes with the tips of her fingers.

The words on the laptop screen had started to blur. One more cup of coffee, and she'd send herself into cardiac arrest from caffeine overdose.

Truth was, she didn't have a clue what to do next.

She'd combed over the notes half a dozen times. After five interviews of her own and more than a dozen from her deputies, they were no closer to finding the Cabbot kids. Anyone who had made her internal radar beep even a little seemed to have a solid alibi.

Owen and Alicia Cabbot's anniversary was an open secret. More than ten people had seen them at the restaurant and confirmed they were a bit tipsy when they left for home.

The pastor's neighbor, Mrs. Willis, had indeed noted his ancient black Lincoln Town Car pulling into the driveway just before midnight. Wagoner hadn't left home again, she said, because she'd have noticed. Mrs. Willis was such a busybody that Marilyn had believed her absolutely.

Even Valetti, Billy's science teacher, was off the list of possible suspects. Not because he was with his buddy CJ, who had landed a few hours ago in Mexico. CJ hadn't seen Valetti last night at all.

Instead, Valetti had spent the night with the very married school gym teacher. Once his lover heard about Emily, she called and set the record straight.

When Marilyn confronted him with the truth, he'd babbled and apologized profusely for lying. She'd been tempted to lock him up, just to teach the teacher a lesson. But she wanted to devote the energy to finding Billy instead.

Marilyn pushed her chair back from her desk and stood, wincing as she realized her left foot had fallen asleep. She needed to do something. Time was running short. Sitting behind this desk made her feel beyond helpless.

She'd assign a second set of eyes to these interviews and then she'd get back out there.

Beat the bushes. Talk to more people, go back to the Cabbots one more time.

She was missing something. She had to be.

And Billy Cabbot's chances were shriveling faster than a worm in the sun.

"Brady's checking in with the parole officer of every registered sex offender in the area. Maybe we'll get a hit." Marilyn said when she placed the stack of interviews on Pippa's desk. "Sit and read through every line of these interviews again, will you? Make sure we haven't missed something."

"Absolutely. One word at a time. I swear." Pippa nodded. "What are you going to do,

Sheriff?"

"I'm going to stop back at the Cabbots and see if they've

thought of anything new that could help." The plan sounded desperate even in her own ears, but Pippa, bless her, didn't say so. Instead, she bowed her head to the task as if she hadn't already reviewed the interviews a dozen times.

Marilyn collected her equipment on her way to the parking lot. The evening news reporters had already swarmed in like vultures and she also wanted to take the time to talk to the family about what they should say and what they might want to keep to themselves.

She stepped out into the evening heat and climbed into the scorching bench seat when her phone rang. She hit the green button to accept the call without looking at the screen.

"Sheriff Pleva."

"Marilyn, it's Jess Kimball." The no-nonsense tone cut through the line. "How are things going with the missing boy? My case here in Austin is winding up. I should be done tomorrow afternoon. I could be there before dinner time if you need me."

"I appreciate that more than you know." She resisted the reality that Billy might be out there, scared and in danger, for another night. Or worse.

She squeezed the bridge of her nose between her thumb and forefinger in an attempt to ward off the coming migraine. No time for that. She had a boy to find and a girl to avenge.

"I'd welcome the help, Jess."

"Will do. What've you got so far?"

Marilyn ran through the new details of the case, including even the most mundane information. Every law enforcement officer knew that the details were important in a situation like this one. Criminals who overlooked the small things were the ones who got caught.

"I keep thinking how awkward it must have been for the kidnapper to manage two kidnappings at once without waking the Cabbots, you know?" Jess cut in as she was winding down. "Is it possible the kids left home on their own? Maybe ran into trouble once they were out of the house?"

"We've checked. We haven't found anyone who saw them wandering around." Marilyn shook her head, although Jess couldn't see her. "It's possible, but these kids were well loved. Good in school. No reason to believe they ran away."

She heard Jess take a deep breath on the other end of the line. "Unless they knew him.

Went with the kidnapper willingly."

Marilyn's shoulders slumped. This was the conclusion she didn't want to reach. "So far, every one of the alibis have checked out. Every name the parents gave us and everyone else we could turn up on our own. No one unaccounted for."

"And you're sure the parents are not involved?" Jess almost whispered.

"As sure as we can be at this point, I guess."

Jess sounded relieved, and stronger. "So what about someone a little more distant, but the kids would still recognize?"

"I've checked everyone I can think of. Got someone specific in mind?"

"I'm thinking back to another child kidnapping case I covered a few years ago. The Central Florida Child Killer."

"I remember that one. He only took boys, didn't he?"

"That's right. Cops thought the killer had to be someone known to the kids. But they couldn't find him."

"Okay," Marilyn said, because Jess wouldn't waste her time.

"Thing was, once they found the guy, and figured out his

background, it turned out he did kind of know the kids. The parents, too. And everyone else in their small community. He wasn't close a friend, really. Turned out they were members of the same church." Jess paused. "There was a sense of trust. The kids didn't exactly know the guy, but they knew who he was. And they had no reason to fear him."

Marilyn nodded. Made sense. Most criminals weren't masterminds. They simply took advantage of the opportunities presented to them.

"The connection turned out to be a church. Could have been a bowling league or a traveling soccer team. Anything like that where people were familiar but not inside the kids' immediate circle." Jess took a deep breath. "It's a long shot, but you could check the sex offenders and violent criminals against a list of members. If the kids or the parents were involved with any groups like that."

Marilyn let the thought roll around in her mind for a second. Emily and Billy were old enough to be involved with more than a single science fair, surely. Owen and Alicia were friendly people. They owned a local business. Maybe Rotary members or quilt clubs or even reading groups.

"Thanks, Jess." She nodded, slowly. "Can't hurt to try. In groups like that, everybody could have known the Cabbots were celebrating their anniversary. Most folks around here know Owen Cabbot, in particular, drinks more than he should. That he'd be sleeping off the booze that night after they got home. It's possible."

"Good. Check it out. If I think of anything else, I'll call you. Otherwise, I'll see you tomorrow," Jess said. "Keep me posted."

"Will do."

Marilyn hung up and popped her car into reverse. She dialed

Pippa's number and tasked her with finding a list of the groups where any of the Cabbots might have been members. She explained why.

"You got it, Sheriff," Pippa said, ever ready to do whatever needed to be done. No doubt about it, Pippa was a keeper, Marilyn thought as she disconnected.

She'd planned to stop at the Cabbots' first, but that could wait. With Jess's suggestions fresh in her mind, she pulled off Main Street and took the turn to Chapel Hill Road toward the Cabbots' church.

She knew many members of the small congregation. A third of them were people she'd already interviewed today. Maybe more. But she hadn't cast a wide enough net.

She needed the full membership list.

Although she'd passed by the place several times a week, she'd never been inside the small country church. She swung the big Ford into the lot and slid it into park.

The pastor's home was adjacent to the church. She noted his car was in the driveway and his porch light was blazing. Sure enough, when she glanced across the street, Mrs. Willis was peeking through her kitchen curtain. Marilyn grinned. Pastor Wagoner probably didn't get away with much.

She unbuckled her seatbelt and left the car, cell phone in hand. As she covered the walkway, she scrolled for Owen Cabbot's home number, just as she climbed the four steps to the porch. She paused while she made the call.

"Hello," a solemn, male voice murmured into the receiver. He sounded totally sober, which he probably was.

"Owen? It's Sheriff Pleva. I'd like to stop by in a few minutes. I've got a couple of questions I need you to help me with. Okay?"

"Yes, yes, that's fine. We certainly won't be sleeping any time soon." He sounded hollowed out, like if a hard wind blew, it would suck him away with it.

No words would give him comfort, no platitude would make a dent in his grief, so she simply muttered, "Okay, I'll see you soon."

She dropped the phone into her pocket and raised her hand to rap on the door when a noise coming from the back yard caught her ear.

She strained to identify it.

Spraying water?

Why would anyone spray water back there at night?

She picked her way around the side of the house and called out, "Pastor Tim?" "Yes?" He sounded wary.

She rounded the corner and he came into view. Sky blue pajamas hung on his lean frame and a pair of glasses perched on the end of his nose. He turned off the hose nozzle and eyed her with surprise. "Marilyn. I didn't hear you knocking. Sorry. Please, come in."

He quickly rolled the hose up around its wheel and gestured an open palm toward the stairs to the back deck.

"No need for that, I'll only take a minute. Sorry to disturb you at all, really." She offered an apologetic shrug for the interruption. "I need to get a list of church members to interview about the Cabbot kids."

"Well, I must say, that is a disturbing request. You think one of our members has done this?" He frowned and motioned toward the stairs again. "Are you sure you won't come in? I was just about to pour myself some Earl Grey and work on my sermon. I can place a quick call to Mrs. Byers, the church secretary, and have her email us the list."

"The Cabbots are expecting me and I don't want to keep them waiting. If you can forward the list to me," she reached into her back pocket and tugged out a business card, "as soon as she gets it to you, I'd appreciate it. We're still looking for Billy. We have to make sure we check everywhere."

He nodded and took the card, face full of despair. "I brought supper to Alicia and Owen earlier this evening and we prayed together again. I'm hopeful the Lord will see fit to return their son."

"Yes, that's what we all hope for," Marilyn said. "Thanks again for your help."

"And thank you for all of your hard work, Sheriff."

She turned and picked her way through the cluttered yard as he headed up the back stairs. She was almost to her car before she noticed the entire lawn was dry and brown.

She cocked her head. Hadn't he been standing there with the hose on?

She replayed the scene in her mind.

She'd walked around to the back. The ground was nothing more than rocks and cracked, dry earth. Not even a patch of succulents that would need watering.

She shivered.

This case was making her both punchy and paranoid.

On the other hand, well-honed instincts were every good cop's stock in trade. Hers had saved her life more than once. She wasn't about to ignore them now.

Could be nothing.

Probably was nothing.

She squared her shoulders. She could take two extra minutes to go check it out, or she might look back at this moment with regret forever.

She retraced her steps, feeling somewhat foolish. She reached for the flashlight on her belt, but with the high hanging moon, she didn't need it.

She circled the yard quietly and found no obvious sign of plants or water anywhere.

So what was he doing with the hose?

She glanced around the area. How far was she going to take this?

She had no warrant to search the pastor's property. She could search anyway, but whatever she found might not be admissible in court. Assuming she found any evidence at all.

The safest thing to do was knock on his door and ask him the inane question, "What exactly were you watering?"

She drummed her fingers restlessly on the butt of the flashlight. Which was when she heard it.

A low, repetitive *bang* rang out from an old shed in the corner of the lot. She stepped closer, shifting her hand from her flashlight to unsnap her holster.

"Hello? Who's there?" she called, as she crept toward the wooden structure. "Police.

Show yourself."

She moved toward the noise, growing louder as she approached.

"Sheriff?"

She wheeled around to find Wagoner standing behind her, brows drawn. "Did you forget something?"

"As I was leaving, I heard a noise back here. I wanted to make sure you didn't have an intruder."

Another *bang* sounded and the pastor's face broke into a relieved smile.

"Oh, that. You scared me there for a second. I've been

dealing with raccoons for the past two months trying to get into my compost pile through a hole under the floorboards." He pointed to the corner of the shed where the banging seemed to originate. "I set up a couple of cage traps. Sounds like they've taken the bait and sprung the trap again. Once they get inside, they really beat themselves up trying to get out. What a racket they can make."

She moved her hand from her pistol to her flashlight as she took another step closer to the shed.

"Well then, it's your lucky day," she said, forcing a tight smile. "I can drop the trap off for you at animal control on the way back to the station."

She grabbed her flashlight and flipped it on as she approached the shed door. She fingered the padlock and sent Pastor Tim a quick glance. "You have the key someplace handy?"

"Yes," he said, gesturing to a rock by her feet. "Underneath that stone. This is where we keep the church's landscaping equipment and it took us the better part of last summer to raise enough funds to buy the mower."

Everything he'd said was plausible. Yet, the small hairs stood up on the back of her neck and gooseflesh covered her arms, even in the warm night.

She kept one eye on Wagoner as she bent to retrieve the key. Which was when she noticed the damp soil at her feet and a darker spot of what could have been blood on the stone.

Her heart kicked against her ribs. She moved her left hand toward the Taser at her hip. "What were you watering in the—"

The blow came fast, a stunning shot to the side of her head with what felt like a brick, only harder. She stumbled forward and then pitched, face first, into the dirt.

Her ears rang.

She struggled up onto all fours.

A second blow connected with her jaw.

She heard the Pastor's voice bark out a low command. "Throw her down there with him before Willis sticks her nose out here."

Marilyn faded in and out of consciousness, clinging to two thoughts.

One filled her with hope. Billy Cabbot might be still alive. He could be in this shed.

One chilled her with abject terror half a moment before he hit her again and she lost consciousness.

CHAPTER FIVE

"WAKE UP," A LOW voice snarled, breaking into the blessed haze of unconsciousness.

A resounding *slap* rang through in her head and her face stung with the contact as her eyes shot open. She blinked furiously, trying to get her bearings.

The scent of sweat and urine and fear rushed in at her and she gagged.

"We can play this two ways. The easy way is you tell me now. The hard way is he beats you until you tell me," Wagoner said, swiping the back of his hand over his sweatslicked face.

She forced herself to pick up her throbbing head to peer beside her. A small, prone form lay just a couple feet away.

"Billy?" she murmured, nearly choking on metallic taste of the blood from a split lip already beginning to swell. "Billy, can you hear me?"

"He's sleeping, if the extra dose didn't kill him," Wagoner said, shooting a pointed glance to the far corner of the ten-by-ten shed.

She followed his gaze. A hulking, ghoulish-looking man stood in the corner, his face pulled into a deep frown. The two didn't look much alike. But something about the shape of their faces and the way they moved was the same.

"Why? Why did you do this?" she mumbled, to keep him talking, to give herself time.

Her tongue felt thick and dry in her mouth. Every second that passed seemed like one closer to the very edge of oblivion. Even sitting upright seemed impossible.

After the blows, the migraine she'd willed away earlier in the day was now a full, hard throbbing in her head.

She glanced at Billy again. He'd shifted restlessly, revealing his face in the moonlight filtering in through the filthy window. His plump cheeks were smeared with dirt and his clothes were soaked through. But damn it, he was alive. And she would do whatever it took to make sure he stayed that way.

"He only wanted to play with Billy," Wagoner said, perhaps by way of apology.

Marilyn's confusion was like thick, gooey molasses inside her pounding head. She tried to grasp his words, but comprehension wouldn't come.

Wagoner still in his pajamas, reading glasses perched on the end of his nose, stood before her with a shovel in hand. He was an almost invisible little man.

But was there a hardness in his eyes? A cruelty around the edge of his mouth?

Had the collar and the Cabbots' friendship with him distracted her from the truth?

Or was her brain so scrambled that she couldn't process the truth?

What was it Jess Kimball had said? About getting two kids

out of the house? She moved her head slowly for another long look at the second man, who stared at her from his spot in the corner.

He looked like Wagoner.

And yet, he didn't.

Her vision distorted into multiple bright zigzags, like looking through a turning kaleidoscope, and nausea swirled in her belly.

"So you drugged them before bedtime and left the window open." The kaleidoscope scrambled and the nausea grew.

She took deep breaths and closed her eyes a moment. The kaleidoscope played out on her closed eyelids, which was worse, so she popped her eyes open again.

"I wish I had. Emily would still be alive if I'd drugged her. Tony wanted to play with Billy." Wagoner shook his head. "I didn't know he'd left the window unlocked. He climbed back into the house after the Cabbots passed out."

"Who's Tony?"

"Me!" The big man in the corner shouted, as if the question was a game. "Me, Tony!" Marilyn narrowed her right eye and turned her head slightly and gazed across the shed only through her left eye, to avoid the kaleidoscope. "You're Tony?"

"Yes!" he shouted. The volume sliced through her head like a guillotine.

"What happened to Emily?" Marilyn asked, as quietly as possible. Maybe if she spoke quietly, Tony would, too.

"Emily fell." Tony dropped his chin to his chest. "Billy got mad."

Marilyn's scrambled brain seemed to clear, like a brief parting of dark clouds during a storm. She glimpsed an important insight.

Tony was the key to this case, not Tim.

Pastor Wagoner wasn't a killer. She hadn't misjudged him that badly.

Tony was the guilty one.

She formed a cautious plan without taking her one-eyed gaze from Tony.

Speaking quietly and calmly, she said, "My deputy will be here soon, Tim. Cut your losses and go while you still can. You've got one murder on you already." "Liar," he snapped.

But he wasn't certain, because in her periphery, his hands fisted as he turned to peer through the dirty window.

"Just go. Now. For Tony's sake. Before something happens to him." She sensed that Tim's bond with Tony was stronger than anything else she could grasp hold of right now.

Tim didn't reply.

Marilyn tried another angle. "Leave Billy here with me. I'll see he gets home. Alicia and Owen will be so happy to have him back. You are their pastor. It's your duty to comfort them, Tim."

She swallowed hard and inched her hand toward her hip.

Her holster was empty.

Carefully, she glanced around the small shed.

"I wouldn't if I were you," Wagoner said when her eyes lit on her pistol resting on a workbench. "He'd bash your head in like a pumpkin on Halloween. He'd have already shot you with it if that old biddy across the way would ever mind her own business."

The last piece of the puzzle clicked into place a split second before her pulse kicked in to high gear.

"Tony, hand me that cloth please," Wagoner said.

Tony creaked into action, fiddling in the corner with a bottle and a cloth. He shuffled toward Wagoner, one hand outstretched, the other pinching his nose like a child.

The distinctive astringent smell preceded him by three yards. Chloroform.

If he got close enough to hold chloroform over her face, she was as good as dead and so was Billy.

She slapped her palms over her ears as she sucked in deep a breath and let out an earpiecing scream. Her head felt as if it might cleave in two and splat her brains all over the dirt floor.

Wagoner lunged toward her.

She rolled to the side.

Her distorted vision made it impossible to aim.

She screamed and kicked out hard and fast with both legs until her booted heel connected squarely with the most vulnerable spot on the outside of his right knee.

She felt the tendons and then the bones give with a sickening pop and tear, like pulling the legs off a giant turkey at the joints.

He howled with the searing pain and went down, crabbing frantically sideways out of kicking range.

Tony dropped the chloroform-soaked cloth and let out a roar.

He grabbed a shovel and raised it high above his head, eyes wild, furious.

She used the last of her ebbing strength to lunge forward and close her hand over the butt of her pistol.

The next moments passed in that zone where actions were fast and her mind was slow.

Tony came straight at her like a charging bull.

Big, broad target.

Easy aim.

Slow, steady squeeze.

Explosive blast.

Kick jolt to her wrist.

Scent of gunfire.

Shots reverberating in her ears.

Her arm fell to her side.

Her head might literally explode at any moment.

The kaleidoscope distortions to her vision heightened the nausea. She held back a heave.

She stared at Tony. He'd staggered away from the blast before he hit the floor.

Behind him, to the right, lay Wagoner, prone on the ground, holding his ruined leg and keening. Blood flowed from a gash on his head. His right leg was bent at a totally unnatural angle.

Her head felt heavy on her neck. She strained to keep her chin up. Kaleidoscopes distorted her vision in both eyes now, but she didn't dare look away or drop her weapon.

CHAPTER SIX

SHE'D LOST ALL TRACK of time before a low, male voice sounded, as if it came from a mile away.

"Marilyn? Can you hear me?" Dimly, she recognized her deputy, Brady Colton. He took hold of her arm and squeezed it gently. "You're going to be okay."

She nodded, the motion sending a knife of pain through her skull. "Billy?"

Brady knelt beside the little boy and pressed two fingers to his neck. Marilyn sucked in a breath.

Brady's relieved gaze connected with hers. "He's still alive."

Alive. Thank God.

Her vision flickered and then went black.

CHAPTER SEVEN

"I WILL NEVER GET used to that," Jess Kimball said quietly as they watched the Cabbots toss a rose on their daughter's coffin.

Marilyn blinked away glassy tears and nodded. "I think that's for the best. The second we start thinking a coffin like that is part of the norm, we might as well pack it in." "Amen," Jess murmured.

The sun had sizzled away the early morning fog, leaving behind another blistering hot day. Marilyn shivered.

It had been four days since she'd found Billy in the shed and two since she was released from the hospital, but the horror of it clung to her like oil on her skin. Whenever she closed her eyes, she saw Tony's face, and her stomach bottomed out.

So close. They'd been so close to losing Billy, it hurt to think about.

Jess nodded toward Mrs. Willis. "She's on her way over."

"That's good. I haven't had a chance to thank her yet. Without her, Billy and I would both be dead."

Mrs. Willis had seen Marilyn arrive, walk around the house,

head to her car, then turn and skulk around to the back yard a second time. She'd called the station, alerting the deputies. Brady, ever diligent, arrived just in time to handle the cleanup.

"Marilyn, dear." The older woman gave her arm an affectionate squeeze. "I'm so glad you're up and around again. Billy, too."

"Thank you, Mrs. Willis." Marilyn patted her hand. "You're the one who saved Billy's life by mere minutes. If you hadn't called Brady—"

When the paramedics had reached the scene, Billy's blood pressure was ninety over sixty and dropping, due to whatever drugs Tony had administered.

Billy was recovering, but not well enough to attend his sister's funeral. Which Marilyn felt was for the best. He blamed himself. Tony had wanted to see Billy's rocket for the science fair that night. Billy had wanted to demonstrate. But Emily tried to stop them.

Mrs. Willis offered a shaky smile. "I wish I could have helped Emily, too."

"I wish we both could have." Marilyn shared a sad glance with her and nodded before Mrs. Willis moved on.

When Mrs. Willis was out of hearing range, Jess said, "Emily fell, just like Tony claimed, you know. The medical examiner confirmed. The evidence is consistent with a fall down those steep stairs from her bedroom. It's a wonder her parents didn't hear her. I'm sure they'll never forgive themselves, although they couldn't have saved her life, even if they'd heard."

Marilyn felt a rush of sympathy. Every time Jess saw something like this, it had to chip away at her. Her face was tense, her eyes full of grief, and Marilyn wondered if her suffering wasn't worse than the Cabbots' in its own way. Jess clung to the hope, no matter how slim, that her son Peter was out there somewhere. But the relentless pressure of never knowing must be crushing her every day.

Marilyn cleared her throat and rotated her stiff jaw. "Want to go get a cup of coffee before you catch your flight back?"

"Let's do that. I forgot to ask this morning. Did Wagoner confess?"

"He filled in most of the missing pieces," Marilyn nodded. "He claims Tony had been at the Cabbot house with them all night. Tony liked the kids and Billy in particular. But they'd concealed Tony's presence because of the parents. Both Owen and Alicia were afraid of him. Didn't want him around the kids."

Jess said, "Parents have good instincts where their kids are concerned. They were right."

"Tony was Tim Wagoner's younger brother. He was mentally handicapped. Sly and cunning, but low IQ." Marilyn paused for a breath. "Wagoner says it was Tony who went back to the Cabbot house that night. Tony who climbed in the window he'd left open earlier in the evening. He said Emily's death was an accident. He claimed she fell before he figured out where Tony was and made it back to the house."

"What about the truck stop? Why leave Emily there?" Jess asked.

"Wagoner said he thought no one would find the body back there until he had a chance to bury her." Marilyn shook her head. "If that truck driver hadn't stumbled in the wrong direction while looking for the men's room, Wagoner would have been right."

"Your crime techs found hair and fibers and other forensics in the trunk of Wagoner's black Town Car. Enough to prove that both kids were stashed in that trunk. And a few matching trunk fibers on Emily's clothes, to confirm." Jess cocked her head.

192 | DIANE CAPRI

After a few seconds, she said, "I guess we'll never know for sure. It's not like Tony can contradict his brother now."

"I don't believe it. I think Wagoner is more involved than he admits. For one thing, why was his hat still inside the house?" Marilyn shook her head. "But his lawyer worked out a plea deal. He confessed to the kidnapping and covering up the crimes, in exchange for life in prison without possibility of parole."

"He lost his brother. And he'll spend the rest of his life in prison." Jess shook her head slowly.

Marilyn replied, "But none of that will bring Emily Cabbot back to life or erase the guilt from Billy's heart. It does nothing to repair Owen and Alicia's ruined lives, either."

Jess and Marilyn watched the Cabbots say their last goodbyes to their beloved daughter.

"I wish we could, but we can't save them all," Jess said, giving her arm a squeeze. "Saving Billy and giving the Cabbots closure for Emily will have to be enough this time."

Marilyn knew Jess meant she craved closure for her son. Marilyn hoped that one day, Jess would find Peter, too.

THE END

JACK
IN THE GREEN

Thank you to some of the best readers in the world:
Natalie Chernow, Angie Shaw (Noah Daniel),
Dan Chillman (Danimal), Lynette Bartos (Derek Bartos),
Teresa Burgess (Trista Blanke) for participating in our
character naming giveaways which make this book
a bit more personal and fun for all of us.

Perpetually, to Lee Child, with unrelenting gratitude.

CAST OF PRIMARY CHARACTERS

Kim L. Otto
Carlos M. Gaspar

Thomas Weston
Samantha Weston
Steven Kent

Jessica Kimball
Jennifer Lane
Willa Carson

Charles Cooper
Jacqueline Roscoe

and
Jack Reacher

The Killing Floor
by Lee Child
1997

I thought: should I be worried? I was under arrest. In a town where I'd never been before. Apparently for murder. But I knew two things. First, they couldn't prove something had happened if it hadn't happened. And second, I hadn't killed anybody.

Not in their town, and not for a long time, anyway.

* * *

"So let's talk about the last twenty-four hours, [Reacher]," he said.

I sighed. Now I was heading for trouble.

"I came up on the Greyhound bus," I said.

"Where did you get on the bus?" he asked me.

"In Tampa," I said. "Left at midnight last night."

"Tampa in Florida?" he asked.

I nodded. He rattled open another drawer. Pulled out a Greyhound schedule. Riffed it open and ran a long brown finger down a page. This was a very thorough guy.

CHAPTER ONE

FBI SPECIAL AGENT CARLOS Gaspar lounged back in the driver's seat of the rental sedan to stretch his bad right leg, but all senses remained fully alert. The last time he'd been on MacDill Air Force Base, Gaspar's partner had been wounded and a man had died resisting routine arrest. It was his sixth sense that rankled. He had a bad feeling about the place. He couldn't shake it.

He'd chosen the center lane and pulled into place behind a line passing steadily through the guard stations. One SUV ahead now, sporting a patriotic car magnet.

Veteran, probably.

Once upon a time, a veteran could be trusted to follow protocol. Veterans knew the rules. Knew they couldn't bring personal weapons on the base or enter restricted areas. They didn't need to be watched. But increasingly, veterans and even active military seemed to be going off the rails now and then.

Sometimes for good cause.

Reacher was a veteran. Gaspar never allowed himself to forget that.

He preferred the smaller Bayshore Gate entrance. Closer to their destination. Less traffic. Only one lane. Only one sentry. Ruled out for just that reason: Because that sentry had fewer vehicles to inspect, she'd be more likely to ask thorough questions Gaspar would not answer. Which would probably land him in the brig and he didn't have time for that today.

The main gate entrance to Tampa's MacDill Air Force Base was less treacherous because he could get lucky. Three traffic lanes fed into the main gate. Each lane supported two security stations configured to more closely resemble drive-through windows at a prosperous suburban bank than a military checkpoint.

Except bank tellers don't wear BDUs and side arms.

Base security handled 20,000 people passing through every day as a matter of routine. Today was not routine. Which meant security would be relaxed, maybe.

From behind aviator sunglasses, Gaspar watched the security process unfold predictably around him. But the whole setup of the event felt wrong. Too much lead time since the target's attendance was announced, for one thing. Too public. Too many people. An unpredictable target with too many enemies and too many secrets.

And the usual dearth of good Intel about everything.

It was a bad combination and he didn't like it, even without factoring Reacher into the equation.

Not that it mattered to the Boss what Gaspar liked or didn't like.

The flashing sign outside the security checkpoint declared Force Protection Condition Alpha, meaning only slightly elevated security in place. Probably bumped up a notch because of expected increased civilian attendance at the annual memorial service honoring deceased members of military families, he figured. He took that as a good omen. The base commander couldn't feel as uneasy as Gaspar did or security would be tighter.

He palmed his plastic VA card and flipped it through his fingers like a Las Vegas card shark, then tapped it rapidly on the steering wheel as if that would encourage the security personnel to speedier service. The Boss said Gaspar's VA card would serve as required military ID to enter the base because of the hundreds of people expected at the memorial ceremony. Gaspar figured the Boss had greased the wheels to make it so, as he usually did.

Gaspar glanced over at his current partner to confirm that she wasn't freaking out any more than usual. "How late are we?"

He'd bought the aviators months ago to block the blinding glare of Miami sunlight. Now, they also served to shield him from her penetrating evaluation of his every move.

His shades weren't needed at the moment, as it happened. "Twenty-five minutes," FBI Special Agent Kim Otto replied, without lifting her gaze from her smart phone's screen.

He'd found Otto's nuanced perception almost telepathic in the weeks since the Boss had paired them up for reasons unknown. They worked well together. He liked her. She seemed to like him well enough. The partnership was improving.

But he was still wary.

Otto's self-preservation instincts never relaxed. Not for half a moment. Ever.

He had a family to support. And twenty years to go. And this was the only field assignment he'd been offered since his disabling injury. Playing second on the team to a woman ten years greener added to the insult. Yet he felt grateful to have the work, mainly because it was the only option he had.

But the Reacher job was more dangerous than they'd been told. Much more. As a result, Otto was jumpier than a mosquito on steroids. She would replace him in a hot second if she became the slightest bit concerned about his reliability.

And she'd be smart to cut him out. He'd do the same to her if their roles were reversed. Maybe even as their roles were now.

So he had to be careful. Safer that way.

Which meant he needed as much distance as he could summon inside the sedan before she sensed any danger.

Why was it so hot in here? He flipped up the fan speed on the air conditioning.

The security staffer took three steps back from the SUV in front of them and the vehicle passed through. Gaspar raised his foot off the brake and allowed the sedan to roll forward until his window was even with the security officer.

Gaspar's window remained closed, following the Boss's explicit instructions.

He held up his photo VA card between his left index and middle fingers, almost like a salute. The card had a bar code on it. If the security guard followed procedure, she'd scan the card. He waited. She did, and waved him through without hassle. The scan was routine. The data should get lost in the mountain of data collected every day. As long as Gaspar did nothing to draw attention to himself, his presence here today should remain undiscovered by the wrong people. He hoped.

He let the sedan roll on through the checkpoint, releasing a breath he hadn't known he'd been holding. If they'd been required to offer FBI badges or answer questions, or if security had searched the sedan, everything would have become a lot more complicated. His life was already complicated enough.

As much as they relied upon the Boss's promise of lax security in their case, he felt Otto's disapproval emitting like sonar waves. How many other VA cards had been waved through today? Was Reacher's one of them? And who checked the civilians required only to show their drivers' licenses for this special event?

But they'd passed the first hurdle. They were on base. Unidentified. So far, so good.

CHAPTER TWO

THE BOSS HAD SAID their movements would be unrestricted inside the gate. Except for certain areas where armed guards were posted. It would be easy enough to avoid those.

"Notice anything worrisome since you were here last?" Otto asked.

He glanced her way. She had her head turned to look out her window, scanning for threats, probably. Especially from behind, she looked like a tiny Asian doll. The top of her deceptively fragile-looking shoulder rested well below the bottom edge of the big sedan's window. If she hadn't put that alligator clamp on her seatbelt at the retractor, it could have sliced her head off her neck in an accident.

"Well?" she said, more insistent this time, scanning through the front windshield now. When he still didn't reply, she glanced his way.

He shrugged, combed his hair with splayed fingers, turned his head and made a show of looking around.

MacDill Air Force Base was both a country club for military families and a war zone. A strange combination of all-inclusive resort and weaponized death star. It boasted a beach and golf course and a full-featured campground for veterans dubbed "Famcamp," where his last trip here had ended in disaster. Inside the buildings you'd find standard Government Issue everything.

Then there were the heavily armed guards protecting the strategic commands that earned the base its lofty importance to national defense and control over state-of-the-art killing machines around the world.

Before his injury, Gaspar brought his kids to the annual MacDill AirFest. He'd been here on special assignments while he was in the army, and once or twice since he'd been assigned to the FBI's Miami Field Office. He hoped today's arrest would go more smoothly than his last one here.

"It's a simple question, Chico," Otto said, continuing her recon.

"Wish I had a simple answer." He took in the view through the glass again—right, left, front and in the rear view mirror—seeking any unfamiliar additions to the geography.

The base consumed every inch of the small peninsula jutting out into Tampa Bay. The last time he'd been here it was to attend a retirement dinner in the officers' club, which had since been demolished. Nothing abnormal in that. When new facilities were required, it generally meant old stuff was demolished and replaced.

Today's event was a perfect example. Hundreds of civilians were expected at a temporary outdoor stage like it had always been there. The chosen site was close to the Strategic Operations Command Memorial Wall honoring the fallen. Nearby, multiple command centers for war. Death and life combined in paradise, to jarring effect.

"What time is Weston scheduled to be arrested?" he asked.

"After the service," she said, checking her Seiko. "Maybe three hours from now. Plenty of time to get what we came for and get out before the arresting agents move."

"Plenty of time for all sorts of things to happen." He shrugged as if unconcerned, but figured she knew better.

Building a current file on Jack Reacher—filling in the blanks after he'd left the Army's 110th Special Investigations Unit—had seemed routine initially. Until they read the background file, which was thin. Too thin. Since, they'd been pulling the scabs off old wounds Reacher had caused. It meant infiltrating enemy territory every time. Both Gaspar and Otto had fresh scars to prove it.

No reason to believe Weston would be an easier interview subject than the others had been. In fact, from what they'd learned about the man, there was every reason to believe he'd be worse.

They'd been warned to watch out for Reacher, who came, destroyed and departed like a liger. Neither he nor Otto needed to be reminded to watch for him, but Gaspar wanted to believe it unlikely Reacher would try to get Weston today. Their feud was sixteen years old and surely even Reacher might have lost track of Weston in all that time.

"Weston has stayed out of Reacher's way all this time," Otto said. "So why is Weston sticking his neck out by attending this particular memorial ceremony? He could have come any time. The base holds these generic memorials for military family members to pay their respects every year. Weston contacted them a month ago and said he wanted to attend this particular service. It doesn't make any sense, does it?"

"Not to me," Gaspar replied. "So we do what we do."

"Meaning what?"

"Meaning we stay alert. We're missing something important, Sunshine."

Her tone was hard in reply. "So what else is new?"

Gaspar parked the sedan an assured clear distance from civilian traffic around the memorial site, which seemed to have a disproportionate number of handicapped parking spaces, and they stepped out into the warm November sunshine.

Gaspar stretched like a lizard. After the past few weeks in frigid cold, he'd forgotten how good Florida sunshine could feel a few days before Thanksgiving.

Otto watched him from just over the hood of the sedan, but said nothing.

When he stepped around the car, they began walking toward the memorial site, keeping a few yards' distance from other early arrivals. Some were in wheelchairs. Some moved jerkily on new prosthetic limbs. One mystery solved: the excess of handicapped spaces. The memorial service was an annual event to honor fallen members of military families. Many attendees were wounded veterans themselves.

Gaspar's limp was pronounced at first, but eased with exercise, as it usually did.

"I know you're running through it again in your head," Gaspar said with a grin to distract her from his limping. "Just verbalize for me while you're at it. Another run-through never hurts."

She scowled as if he'd falsely accused her. He hadn't. She never stopped thinking, analyzing, crunching data in her head, even if it was the same data, over and over. He didn't complain. Her odd habits had already saved his ass more than once.

"The subject is retired Army Lieut. Col. Alfred Weston." She rattled off the few important facts they'd received in the

Boss's materials: "Sixteen-plus years ago, Weston was posted here on a classified assignment. No details in the file. Weston's wife and three children were murdered. Reacher somehow became the lead Army investigator on the case. He thought Weston was the killer."

"Why?"

"Who knows?" she said, as if she was slightly irritated at Reacher's unfathomable behavior. Which she probably was.

"But Reacher couldn't prove Weston did it," Gaspar continued for her, "and it turned out the real shooter was arrested quickly by the locals." He fingered the Tylenol in his pocket. He'd swallow another one when she wasn't watching. His doctors prescribed narcotic pain medication, but he couldn't risk taking it. Tylenol was the strongest thing he'd allow himself while they were working.

She said, "After the killer's arrest, the official investigation of Weston ended."

"Unofficially, Reacher wouldn't let it go," Gaspar went on. Reacher never let anything go once he had his teeth into it. Otto was the same way. For sheer bulldog tenacity, Reacher and Otto were as alike as bookends.

"Weston's been living abroad," Otto said, "Middle East mostly, since he left the Army under a cloud of Reacher's making." She stopped talking abruptly, as if she didn't want to mention the rest.

Gaspar's right leg was feeling stronger. The cramping easing. Limp nearly under control. Pain ever-present, sure, but he could handle pain. He'd been handling it a good long while.

"And now," Otto said, "Weston's accused of major crimes against the U.S. Government. Various forms of corruption, mostly, related to the private security company he operates. A few allegations of using unauthorized force and excessive force. Suspected manslaughter of civilians is at the center of it. A lot of conflicting evidence. Nothing actually proved so far, but plenty to support an arrest and interrogation." She hesitated half a breath. "This is the first time Weston's been on American soil in the past sixteen years."

Same facts he'd memorized on the plane. He hadn't missed anything. He still didn't like it.

Gaspar mulled for a couple more steps before he asked, "Why come back at all? He's got nothing here. Why not just stay offshore and make Uncle Sam send covert operations after him if we wanted him badly enough?"

She shrugged as if the answer didn't matter, when Gaspar knew it did.

"Once they snatch him," she said, "he'll be locked up and off limits to us. We need to get to him today." She took another breath and glanced again at the plain Seiko on her narrow wrist. "We've got less than an hour before the service starts."

Gaspar felt his eyebrows knitting together. Their mission still wouldn't make sense. "Why should Weston tell us anything useful?"

"The Boss says Weston blames Reacher for his troubles and wants to even the score. We're supposed to give Weston that chance and strongly encourage him to take it." Unconsciously, perhaps, she patted her gun under her blazer.

"We're striking out with Reacher's friends so we'll squeeze his enemies instead?" A harsh, dry chuckle escaped Gaspar's lips. "Sounds a little like sticking your head in the mouth of a hungry carnivore doesn't it?"

Otto said nothing.

CHAPTER THREE

THEY'D BEEN ALLOTTED ONE hour to get in, get what they could, and get out without crossing paths with the arresting agents or stepping in another pile of stink from unknown origins. Flight and traffic delays had sucked up more than half of their time already.

"Your gun's loaded, right?" she said, patting hers again as if she didn't realize she'd touched it.

"Come on, Sunshine." He ran both hands through his hair again and stuffed them in his trouser pockets. "We've been over this. We can't discharge weapons we're illegally carrying. Do you have any idea what would happen if we did that?"

"I'm familiar with procedures," she snapped.

"And you're familiar with prison sentences, too."

She seemed unimpressed with his reasoning. "Weston's made enemies here and around the world. A few have a strong appetite for vengeance."

Gaspar knew she was worrying about one particular enemy. So was he.

"Unlikely Reacher knows Weston's here," he said. "How

would he have heard? The man's far enough off the grid even the Boss can't find him. Not likely anyone else can."

Finding Reacher wasn't the issue, though. The question was whether Reacher would find Weston. Or them—a growing possibility, the longer they went looking for him. Reacher had friends. By now, smart money said at least one of those friends had somehow passed along that they were on his trail.

"Reacher lives to piss on the other guy's grave," Otto said. "He's a highly qualified sniper. The only non-Marine to win the 1000-yard invitational rifle competition."

"It would be crazy to try to kill Weston here where he'll be so heavily guarded. A good sniper would choose a highway location. Shoot from a vehicle. Make a clean getaway," Gaspar said.

Again her hand passed over the lump in her blazer. "I'm saying we need a Plan B. Guns work for me. Unless you've got a better plan."

He didn't.

They'd arrived at the ceremony site. Setup was completed and the audience was slowly filing in. Gaspar estimated seating for about 1,000 people. A temporary, elevated stage at the front, a center podium flanked by four chairs on either side. He saw flat, open parking lots behind the stage where official vehicles and emergency personnel waited. A dark sedan pulled in from the opposite side of the parking lot. Which meant there was a second means of ingress and egress to the area.

One more entrance or escape route to cover. Not ideal.

He studied the site's perimeter. Otto was right. Weston's tenure here at MacDill, and with the Army in general, had produced more enemies than most men accumulated in a lifetime. Yet, today Weston would stand in an open field on an elevated stage surrounded by too many spots for a moderately good shooter to hide.

It felt foolhardy to Gaspar. Weston had to feel the same way.

Any military man would.

Which was one of the things that made the setup feel so profoundly wrong.

Gaspar identified the most likely shelter points for snipers within a seventy yard range. Any military sniper was reliable at five times that distance. There were several good ones and a few more that a sniper as good as Reacher could use to kill and disappear before anyone found his nest. What they had learned about Reacher was that even though he could kill from a distance at any time, he preferred to handle his problems up close and personal. Gaspar had felt like prey every day since he'd received the Reacher assignment. The only reasonable solution was to ignore it and press on.

The base held plenty of weapons and ammo and legitimate personnel who were trained to use them. In theory, all arms were accounted for and all non-security personnel were prohibited from possessing personal weapons on base. In theory.

Like most theories, that one was obviously unreliable. Gaspar knew for sure that at least two people carrying unauthorized weapons were standing in this precise spot already. Seemed to him more than likely there'd be others.

"You know what worries me?" Otto asked.

He laughed. "Everything worries you, Sunshine."

She glared at him. "Why did Weston agree to attend this ceremony, make himself an easy target?"

"I was just wondering that myself," Gaspar said. "Maybe he's got a death wish."

"Or homicidal intent," she said.

Gaspar didn't argue. Either option was possible.

He again checked the potential sniper points he could identify and pointed them out to her. Shooting into a crowd and hitting only the intended target was not a simple thing, but it wasn't impossible, either. The best locations were in the west, with the sun behind him. Firing out of the sun was every sniper's basic preference.

"Just stay out of the line of fire," he told her. "If my partner is shot and killed on a military base, I'll be buried in paperwork for the rest of my natural lifetime. I've got kids to raise."

"Your concern is touching," she said, just before she slugged him in the bicep hard enough to knock him off balance. He righted himself and hammed it up a little to conceal how easily she could fell him.

"Enough horsing around. Be serious for the next ninety minutes, will you?" she scolded.

She was tiny, but fierce. He admired that about her.

Not that he'd let her know it.

Movement near the stage caught his attention. "There's Weston. Let's go."

He set off toward the opposite side of the venue at a good clip. Otto struggled to keep pace at first and then strode past him until it was his turn to struggle. They closed the distance to the edge of the stage where Weston stood at ground level, flanked by a military escort and two women. The escort would be Corporal Noah Daniel, according to the Boss's instructions.

Twenty feet behind Weston stood three bulky civilians wearing navy business suits, white shirts and rep ties, and thick-soled shoes. These could only be private bodyguards. More holes in the "no guns on base" theory, Gaspar figured.

He slowed so Otto reached their target first, allowing Gaspar time to gather quick impressions of the Weston group.

The older woman was Samantha Weston. She was draped in ridiculous fashion garments that probably came from Paris or Milan without benefit of filtering through American good sense.

She was fortyish. Lanky. Lean. Artfully styled hair. Handsomely well-constructed.

Gaspar could spot skilled plastic surgery and *haute couture* across a dim and crowded Miami ballroom. No detective work required here, though. Mrs. Weston's familiarity with both was revealed by Tampa's brutally honest sunlight.

The younger woman standing slightly behind Mrs. Weston was well groomed but plain. Wholesome. Smallish. About thirty, or a couple of years either side, Gaspar guessed. Dark hair. Short, scrubbed fingernails. Everything about her appearance was professionally no-nonsense.

And something else.

She seemed familiar.

A certain lilt to her nose, crinkles around her eyes as she squinted into the sun, dimple in her chin.

Who was she?

Wife of an acquaintance? Ring-less fingers ruled out that option.

Maybe she resembled a celebrity or even a crime victim from a prior case.

He waited a moment for the information to bubble up. No luck. He couldn't place her.

Next, from behind the aviators he scanned the subject like a full body x-ray machine. Weston's dark suit covered him from turkey neck to shiny, cap-toed shoes. All visible body parts were pathetic. Gaspar's scan noted pasty skin, eye pouches, jowls, tremors. Weston was fifty-five, maybe? But he looked every moment of twenty years older.

The expat life in Iraq as a military contractor suspected of murdering local civilians carried its own unhealthy burdens, sure. In Weston's case, the added pressure of surviving the murder of his wife and children on U.S. soil couldn't be easy. Guilt might have gnawed his organs, maybe. Whatever the cause, he looked like he was being eaten alive.

Otto presented herself to them. "Corporal Daniel. Colonel Weston. Mrs. Weston." She hesitated briefly before reaching out to the unidentified younger woman.

"Jennifer Lane," the woman said, extending her hand for a firm shake with Otto first, then Gaspar. "I'm Mrs. Weston's lawyer."

Instantly, Samantha Weston became more concerning. In Gaspar's experience, only people already in trouble and expecting worse trouble traveled with a lawyer.

"I am FBI Special Agent Kim Otto and this is my partner Special Agent Carlos Gaspar. We'd like to talk to Colonel Weston for a few minutes, if you don't mind."

The expression settling on Weston's face was something close to satisfaction. He didn't smile, exactly. More like a smirk. So Weston had expected them. Or someone like them. Which made Gaspar more uneasy than he already was. Why would Weston anticipate that cops would approach him today? The Boss said Weston's arrest was a sting. Gaspar could dream up a dozen explanations, but none of them were good news.

Corporal Daniel performed as ordered. "Mrs. Weston, Ms. Lane, our base chaplain would like a word with you before we begin," he said, leading Samantha Weston away by a firm forearm grip.

Attorney Jennifer Lane followed her client like a pit bull on a leash.

Gaspar positioned himself facing Weston, better to observe and avoid the sniper positions he'd previously noted. Otto stood to one side, also out of identifiable firing lines. Weston remained an easy target and had to know it, but didn't seem to care.

"Sir, we'll only take a few moments of your time," Otto said. "We're hoping you can help us with some background data about the investigating military police officer on your wife's murder case."

"Reacher," Weston said, as though naming an enemy more heinous than Bin Laden. Then, eagerly, "Is he with you?"

Otto's expression, betraying equal parts horror and astonishment at the very thought, was quickly squelched.

Gaspar hid his grin behind a cough. One mystery solved. Weston meant to lure Reacher here today.

And maybe he had. Gaspar didn't find that option comforting in the least.

"We haven't seen him recently," Gaspar said, truthfully enough. He slouched a little and settled his hands into his trouser pockets because it made him seem friendlier. Gaspar knew many successful interrogation techniques, but none of them worked unless the subject wanted to talk. Most of the problem was making them want to. Once they wanted to tell him everything, witnesses were nearly impossible to shut up.

Disappointed that they hadn't served up his quarry, Weston became more suspicious. "Why are you collecting background on Reacher?"

The half-truth rolled more easily off Otto's tongue after weeks of practice, "We're completing a routine investigation."

"Why?"

"He's being considered for a special assignment."

"Cannon fodder? Road kill?" Weston's sharp retorts came fast. "Those are the only jobs Reacher's fit for."

"Meaning what?" Otto asked, unintimidated.

Weston said, "My wife and children were executed. By cowards. While I was serving my country."

"Nothing to do with Reacher, right?" Otto asked.

Weston's face reddened and his eyes narrowed. "Reacher accused me. He arrested me. I wasn't there to see my children buried. I wasn't there to see my wife buried. I sat in a jail cell instead." He clenched and unclenched his fists at his side. "This is the first memorial service I've ever been able to attend for my slain family. You call that nothing? I sure as hell don't."

"Not unreasonable of Reacher, though," Otto said, detached, cool. "Most people are murdered by someone close to them. Anybody who watches television knows that. Reacher wasn't out of line when he considered you a prime suspect."

Weston's chest heaved. He shifted his slight weight and leaned closer to Otto, towering unsteadily over her. She didn't flinch. She remained the polar opposite of cowed. Gaspar figured Weston wasn't used to having any woman stand her ground with him, much less one nearly half his size.

Weston lowered his voice to a mighty pianissimo and still Otto didn't budge even half an inch. "When Reacher found out he was wrong about me? What did he do?"

Otto lifted her shoulders and opened her palms, unimpressed. "I give up."

Otto's behavior enraged Weston a bit more. He leaned in and all but engulfed her like a vulture's shadow. She didn't move and said nothing.

Then, as if he'd flipped some sort of internal switch, he

released the stranglehold on his fists and relaxed his posture. Regular breathing resumed. Sweat beads on his forehead and above his upper lip glistened in the sunlight. A breeze had kicked up, carrying floral scents from the tropical plants in and around the base. A breeze that any good sniper could easily accommodate.

When Weston spoke again, he sounded almost civil, as if Otto had asked him about nothing more personal than last night's dinner menu.

The guy was a sociopath, Gaspar thought. Clearly. Total nutjob. All the signs were there. He'd seen it too many times before.

"It's unfortunate that Reacher's still alive. If I see him before you do, he won't be. Please tell him that for me." His tone reflected the controlled calm Gaspar recognized as subdued rage. A hallmark of stone cold killers, crazy or not.

Gaspar asked, "Why did Reacher think you killed your family? We haven't seen the whole file. Was there some evidence against you?"

"Ask him next time you see him." Weston folded his hands in front of his scrawny abdomen, miming that he had all the patience in the world to do nothing but humor them.

"Right now I'm asking you."

Attendees had been filing in steadily as they talked and now filled the chairs in the audience as well as on the stage. Again, Gaspar noticed a significant number of disabled men and women. Many of them were young. Too young.

Not much time left.

Weston's satisfied smirk turned up a notch. "You work for Cooper, don't you?"

Hearing him utter the Boss's name was a sharp jab, but Gaspar recognized a classic deflection and refused the bait. Whatever happened after Reacher left the Army, he'd been a good cop. After twenty minutes with Weston, Gaspar was ready to believe anything Reacher reported about Weston on Reacher's word alone.

"Why did Reacher think you'd killed your own family?" Gaspar asked again.

Weston said nothing.

Otto stepped in. "Have you communicated with Reacher since you left the army, Colonel?"

"I've been living abroad."

Otto said, "The globe is a lot smaller than it used to be. People travel."

"Too bad Reacher hasn't been to Iraq." And like that, Weston's control again seemed to snap. "I'd happily kill the bastard. Cooper, too, given the chance."

"What's your beef with the Boss?" Gaspar asked. The guy was crazy, but whatever he thought about the Boss, it was better to find out than get caught napping.

"We all wore the green back then. We were brothers in arms. We were supposed to be taking care of each other. The Army's family, man," Weston said. "You served, didn't you? You've got the bearing. I can smell the green on you. You've gotta know what I mean."

Gaspar did know. He was tempted to make a sarcastic remark about simply surviving being a better outcome than what had happened to Weston's real family. Not to mention the dead and disabled who served under Weston's command. But instead Gaspar said, "Right."

Weston stopped a second to wipe the spittle from the corner of his mouth, to gather himself. When he spoke again, the switch had again been tripped. The controlled calm had returned. "You really don't know, do you?"

"Know what?" Otto asked.

"You can't be that stupid." Weston's lip curled up. The kind of smirk that made Gaspar want to break his face. "Cooper's the biggest snake alive. Always has been. Turn your back and he'll bite you in the ass. Reacher was Cooper's go-to guy. The two of them were behind everything that happened to me."

Gaspar shook his head exaggeratedly, like he'd heard better tales from the Brothers Grimm. "You think Reacher killed your family? On Cooper's orders? Then blamed you?"

"I've had a lot of years to think this through. Cooper and Reacher had a vendetta going against me. It had to be them." He paused, smiling like a demented circus clown. "That's the only possible answer."

Otto intervened. "The hit man said you hired him. He testified you wanted your family killed."

Once again, Weston's agitation resurfaced. The man was like a carnival ride. His face reddened. His eyes narrowed. His lips pressed hard together and he stuck out his chin. "Lies!" he shouted, loud enough for members of the crowd filtering in nearby to hear and turn to stare.

"Close enough for government work," Otto replied without flinching. "You'd been threatened by the gang you tried to rip off. You were told what would happen to your family. You failed to deliver their money. Reacher had nothing to do with any of that."

She didn't mention the Boss had reached out by sending them here today and probably by sending Reacher back then, too. Gaspar wasn't the only one who noticed.

Weston rocked closer and loomed over Otto again. "Little girl, if you were half as smart as you think you are, you'd have stopped believing Cooper's fairy tales long ago." He lifted balled fists and unclenched his hands, reaching toward her. He looked like he wanted to shake her by her slender neck until she stopped breathing.

Gaspar hoped he'd try. Otto would knock Weston on his ass the second he touched her. But all this talk about Reacher had heightened his tension, too. On the way through security, Gaspar had been concerned. Now, he felt wired tight, ready to snap.

Before Weston had a chance to complete his move, Samantha Weston appeared by her husband's side like a defending Valkyrie from nowhere.

When Weston didn't back down, his wife placed a firm hand on his shoulder. "Tom, darling. It's time."

Otto had yet to move so much as an eyelash. She said in her normal voice, "We'll finish our questions after the service, Colonel."

Weston didn't flinch for another full second. Then he shook off his wife's hand, turned, marched toward the stage, climbed the steps and stood, waiting for Samantha to catch up.

Gaspar and Otto watched in silence until both Westons reached their positions on the stage with the other honorees of the day's service, and then continued to watch them.

The breeze had whipped up to gusty bursts. Unpredictable. Which would make a sniper's job harder. Not impossible. Some would consider the wind a worthy challenge. Reacher was probably one of them.

Eyes still forward, Gaspar said, "I'm okay with staying a while. We've got a few hours before our flight. But what do you think he'll say later that he wouldn't say now?"

"Weston's the first person we've met who is willing to tell us anything at all about Reacher. I'm not leaving until I hear every last word I can wring out of him." After a full second or so, she asked, "You think the Boss sent us here to see if Weston could actually pin anything on him and Reacher?"

"I gave up trying to guess the Boss's motives years ago." Gaspar nodded in the direction of the entrance, where two males dressed in FBI-normal stood to one side. "More importantly, what are you planning to tell those guys when they ask who we are and what the hell we're doing here?"

"You'll think of something," she replied, focused now on the tableau playing out on the stage. "Who is that reporter talking to Weston?"

CHAPTER FOUR

THE REPORTER WORE A press pass on a chain around her neck, a video camera slung over her back and a recorder of some sort raised to capture a conversation Gaspar couldn't hear. Weston and his wife spoke with her briefly before the lawyer stepped in and stopped the inquiry. A short verbal exchange between the reporter and Lane, the lawyer, ended when Lane herded the Westons to their seats.

Gaspar wondered again where he had seen that lawyer before. He couldn't place her, but he knew her. He was sure of it.

The reporter raised her camera and snapped a few photos of the entire scene before she walked down the four steps from the stage and onto the path directly toward Otto and Gaspar. When she was close enough, he read her press pass.

Jess Kimball, *Taboo Magazine*.

Odd that *Taboo* would be covering Weston. *Taboo* was in the vein of *Vanity Fair*, its only real competitor. Gaspar had seen both magazines around the house because his wife subscribed. Both covered popular culture, fashion, and current affairs. *Taboo* was newer, a bit edgier, maybe, but covered the same beat.

Retired military officers were neither of the national glossies'
usual subject or audience. Which made Gaspar more curious
instead of less.

Gaspar stepped in front of the reporter before she walked
past. "Ms. Kimball, a moment of your time?"

Her eyes, when she focused on his, were piercingly blue.
Nostrils flared. "Yes?"

"Why is *Taboo Magazine* interested in Colonel Weston?"

"And you are?" Kimball held the last word in a long, hostile
invitation to reply.

"Carlos Gaspar. FBI. This is my partner, Kim Otto."

Kimball considered something for a moment before she
answered. "Sorry to say, I'm no threat to Weston."

"What's your interest?" Gaspar asked again.

"My mission is to make sure victims get justice. Especially
children."

"What does that mean?" Otto asked.

"Ever heard of Dominick Dunne?"

"The *Vanity Fair* reporter who covered all those infamous
trials after his daughter was murdered," Otto replied.

"I covered Weston's case a while ago when the gunman who
killed Weston's family was executed by the State of Florida.
Weston was living in Iraq at the time. No chance to wrap up with
him until now without traveling to a war zone."

Otto asked, "Why did you say 'the gunman'?"

"He pulled the trigger. But he wasn't the reason those kids
and their mom were murdered. We've got Colonel Weston to
thank for that," Kimball said, in the same way she'd have
thanked Typhoid Mary for robust health.

"Weston denies involvement," Otto said, "and no connection
was established."

The ceremony was opened by a chaplain, who began with an invocation. Those in the audience with the physical ability stood and bowed their heads. Many closed their eyes. Immediate, eerie quiet reigned.

Kimball whispered. "The Army's cop got it right at the outset."

"Reacher?"

A woman nearby raised her head and glared toward them. Otto held her remaining questions until the brief invocation concluded and the audience returned as one to their seats.

Normal squirming set a low, baseline volume beneath which Kimball replied. "Weston's family was murdered because of Weston. He's got their blood on his hands. Doesn't matter who pulled the trigger and killed them in their beds."

"You're the reason the Westons brought a lawyer here today, huh?" Gaspar asked.

Kimball shook her head with a sour smile. "More likely the divorce Samantha's lawyer filed yesterday the second they set foot on U.S. soil," she said. "Either way, the Westons have more than me to be worried about."

"Why do you say that?" Otto asked.

"You wouldn't be here without an agenda." Kimball tilted her head toward the entrance where the two agents waited. "More of your tribe over there. I'm guessing it's not an FBI picnic. Weston's about to get his. Finally. You can be sure I'm here to get photos."

Silence settled over the crowd again, except for a few members who were quietly crying. Occasionally, a brain-injured veteran would speak inappropriately. There were too many brain-injured veterans after the long war. They'd become a part of normal civilian life for military families. Another burden for the stalwart to bear with dignity. Everyone ignored the interruptions.

Still at the side of the stage, Otto, Gaspar, and Kimball were the only people standing. Drawing too much of the wrong attention.

Kimball handed Gaspar her card.

"Call me later. I'll fill you in," she whispered and slipped away to join the other reporters seated near the opposite side of the stage. She was well within her equipment's visual and audio range and beyond the reach of FBI interrogation while the memorial service continued.

CHAPTER FIVE

THE AUDIENCE HAD EXPANDED while Gaspar had been preoccupied by Weston and then Kimball. Seating was now filled to capacity and additional attendees stood blocking the aisles and the exits. His sightline to the official vehicles behind the stage was obscured, but he could see enough to confirm they remained in place. He couldn't see whether Weston's limo and bodyguards were still present, but they probably were.

On the stage, all the chairs were occupied now. Both Westons and the chaplain were seated to the right of the podium. The base commander wasn't present, but the resident Army Military Intelligence unit was represented by a one-star Brigadier General Gaspar didn't know seated to the left of the podium with two civilians. Enlarged photos of the individuals—and, in Weston's case, the family—being remembered today rested on easels blocking Gaspar's sightline to the area behind the seated dignitaries. No one else on Gaspar's side of the stage could see back there now, even if they'd been looking.

Which they probably weren't, because the enlarged photographs magnetized attention like flames drew bugs. The portrait that interested Gaspar declared a near-perfect American family. Five Westons gathered around Dad and Christmas tree, dressed in matching holiday plaids. Meredith Weston perched on the chair's arm, her husband's arm around her waist. She looked maybe thirty-five, blonde and tan with typically perfect American teeth suggesting she'd been a well-loved child once. Three children. All resembled their mother. You could tell the teenaged daughter, covered with freckles and hiding braces, would grow into her mother's beauty. Twin boys sporting fresh haircuts and suits that matched dad's were already little men. Fortunately, the boys looked like mom, too. Even back then, Colonel Weston wasn't handsome.

The photos reminded Gaspar of his own family. Four daughters, and his wife very pregnant with his first son. Gaspar loved his family like crazy. He refused to try to imagine life without them.

Weston's family had ended up dead. How could any father possibly do that? Gaspar had never understood it, even as he knew fathers killed their families every day.

An intent-looking uniformed man was moving toward them along the edge of the audience, his gaze scanning the crowd, but returning to Gaspar and Otto. This would be their contact, an Air Force Office of Special Investigations officer assigned to assist the FBI agents in Weston's arrest after the memorial service ended. Otto spotted him, too, and the three of them stepped away at a safe enough distance from the crowd to talk while maintaining a clear view of the parade ground, as well as the stage and surrounding elements.

"Agents Otto and Gaspar?"

They nodded.

"Did you get what you came for from Weston? We might

manage another few minutes before the arrest if you need it."

"Actually—" Otto replied, looking for his name plate.

"Call me Danimal. Everybody does."

"Danimal," she said.

"That's right."

Otto shrugged. "OK, Danimal. I'd like more than just another few minutes with the guy. Two days in a room alone with him, maybe. He knows a lot more than he's telling."

"Sorry. Can't happen," he said. "Happy to spill whatever I know, though. Not that there's much to spill. Reacher was a good cop and he did a good job on the case. He had a good close record on his cases, but he couldn't make it stick against Weston. Everything's in the file. I've read it. We can't release the file, but my boss promised yours that I could answer your questions."

"Not a lot of Army here on base back then, right?" Otto asked. "How was this case Reacher's jurisdiction, anyway?"

"Strictly speaking, it probably wasn't. Weston was on base for a few months on a special assignment. Reacher came down after the murders."

Gaspar asked, "So Reacher wasn't assigned to duty here?"

"No need for Army military police like Reacher. Base security handles everything. In appropriate cases, we coordinate with Tampa P.D. and the local FBI. Sometimes other jurisdictions."

"Weston was Army. What was his assignment?"

"Classified," Danimal said, as if no further comment was necessary.

"Weston lived off base. Why was base security involved in the case?"

"All MacDill security teams have good relationships with

local law enforcement. We work together when our personnel are involved."

Otto said, "Reacher disregarded all the standard procedures, I gather."

He nodded. "Murder of an Army officer's family is not the sort of thing we'd keep our noses out of just because it happened off base."

"Weston and Reacher had a history," Gaspar said. "That have anything to do with Reacher's interest?"

Danimal shrugged. "Weston had a history with everybody who crossed his path. He's not an easy guy. You must have noticed."

Gaspar said, "Wife and three kids shot in the head with a .38 while they slept in their own civilian beds around midnight on a Wednesday. Ballistics on the gunshots?"

"It was the wife's gun. First responders found it on the bed still loosely gripped in her hand. Army wives learn to shoot for self-protection and she was damn good at it. In this case, looks like she didn't get the chance to fire."

"Reacher concluded there'd been no intruder?"

"House was in a good, safe South Tampa neighborhood, but shit happens sometimes."

"Not in this case?" Otto asked.

"Right." He nodded. "No forced entry, no identifiable evidence of a break-in. Front door locked and alarm system activated. Family dog asleep in the kitchen."

"The dog slept through the whole thing?" Gaspar asked.

Danimal nodded. "That's what it looked like."

Gaspar had to agree. Dogs don't sleep through break-ins. Not unless they're drugged, or deaf. Or they know the killer. And sometimes, not even then.

"Say Reacher was right. No intruder," Otto said. "Normal conclusion would be murder suicide. Yet the locals ruled that out and Reacher agreed. Why?"

"No motive, for starters."

Gaspar nodded. Women usually need a reason to kill, even if it's a crazy reason.

"By all accounts, she was a wonderful mother, decent wife to a difficult guy. Kids were great, too. Good students. Lots of friends. No substance abuse."

"All-American family, huh?" Otto asked, glancing again at the photographs on the stage.

Danimal shrugged. "Zero reported difficulties."

Which was not the same thing as no problems, exactly. Gaspar was forming a clearer picture of Reacher's analysis of the crimes. "Suspects?"

"No."

"She have any enemies?"

"None anyone could find."

"How hard did Reacher look?"

Danimal shrugged again. "Not too hard, probably. He knew Weston. We all did. Guy had plenty of enemies. We didn't need to spin our wheels looking for hers."

"Where was Weston at the time of the murders?" Otto asked.

"Alibi was weak from the start," Danimal said. "He claimed he was drinking with buddies at a local strip joint until the place closed."

"Devoted family man that he was. Alibi didn't hold up, though?"

"No confirming surveillance available in those clubs, for obvious reasons. Nobody remembered Weston being there after his buddies left about two a.m."

234 | DIANE CAPRI

Gaspar said, "Meaning Reacher focused on the most obvious suspect."

"Pretty much," Danimal said. "Reacher wanted Weston to be guilty, sure. But the rest of us agreed. Reacher wasn't completely wrong."

"Roger that," Gaspar said.

"What happened next?" Otto asked.

Danimal looked uncomfortable for the first time. "That's a little...vague."

"Let me guess," Otto said, sardonically. "Weston was hauled in looking like he'd been run over by a bus, right?"

Danimal shrugged and said nothing.

"What persuaded Reacher to abandon charges against Weston?" Gaspar asked.

Silence again.

Otto asked, "So what happened after Weston's arrest?"

"Case was over, as far as we were concerned. The situation moved up the chain of command, out of Reacher's purview. He returned to his regular post."

"Where was that?"

"Texas, maybe?" Danimal said.

"But that wasn't the end of things, was it?"

"Pretty quickly, local detectives concluded Weston's family had been killed by a cheap hit man."

"How cheap?" Gaspar asked.

"Five-hundred dollars, I think, for all four hits."

"Anybody could have paid that," Otto said. "Even on Army wages."

Danimal didn't argue. "They couldn't tie Weston to the killer, so charges against Weston were dropped. Reacher had no say in the matter. Even if he'd still been on base, the result would have been the same."

Gaspar said, "Reacher had to love that."

Danimal laughed. "Exactly."

Otto tilted her head toward Jess Kimball, who was still sitting with the press off to the opposite side of the stage. "Reporter over there says Weston's family was killed to send him a message. Any truth to that?"

"Probably. But that made him a victim, not a suspect. We couldn't prove anything more," Danimal replied.

"How hard did you try?" Gaspar asked.

"If the evidence was there, Reacher would have found it. He was a good cop and he did a good job on the case."

After thinking a bit, Otto said, "After Weston was released, Reacher kept looking for evidence, didn't he? And he let it be known. He hounded Weston, figuring he'd crack. Or do something else Reacher could charge him for, right?"

Danimal said nothing.

Otto said, "A few of your guys maybe helped Reacher out with that project."

Danimal still said nothing.

Weston was a scumbag through and through. Reacher wouldn't have let that go. Gaspar wouldn't have, either.

"How'd it end?" Otto asked.

"Weston was arrested frequently. Jaywalking. Spitting on the sidewalk. Whatever," Danimal replied.

"Didn't matter as long as Weston was getting hassled and locked up for something and sporting a few bruises, right?" Otto asked.

He shrugged. "When Weston came up for his next

promotion, he got passed over. His CO suggested he'd be better off outside, away from, uh, constant surveillance."

"So Weston retired," Otto said.

"Yes."

"And then what?"

Danimal replied, "And then he got worse."

Gaspar figured Reacher had been counting on that. Reacher had sized Weston up and concluded he was a scumbag. Guys like Weston don't get better with age.

While Danimal was briefing them, Gaspar had been preoccupied with Reacher and not watching Weston closely enough. For Gaspar's assignment, Weston was a source of information and nothing more. After he told them what they needed to know, Weston could stand in front of a firing squad and Gaspar wouldn't have cared. Because he agreed with Reacher. Weston killed his family, one way or another. Weston was not the victim here.

Until he was.

CHAPTER SIX

THE SERVICE CONCLUDED. THE chaplain returned to the microphone and asked everyone to stand and bow their heads. Weston, his wife, and the others on the stage did so, along with the audience. Hushed whispers from the respectful crowd stopped. The only noises Gaspar heard were muffled by distance. The chaplain began his benediction.

A split second later, the first gunshot shattered the quiet. Automatically, Gaspar's gaze jerked toward the sniper nests he'd located—was that a rifle's glint he saw snugged up against that HVAC unit?—then back to the stage. He counted two more rapid shots. Like a crazy break dance, Weston's body lurched forward, propelled by the force of each impact from behind, not from any identified nest. Had Gaspar imagined the rifle's glint?

After the third shot, Weston crumpled like a marionette whose strings were abruptly severed.

When Weston fell, he opened a window for the fourth shot, which hit Samantha Weston.

The fifth bullet struck the chaplain.

Gaspar and Otto were already rushing the stage with their

weapons drawn after the third shot, but their sightline behind the stage was still obscured. They'd left Danimal behind with his own weapon drawn, scanning the crowd for the shooter as he got on his radio.

Like a brief time delay on live television, the audience began screaming and chaos erupted just as Otto reached the stage with Gaspar half a step behind. As Gaspar followed her around the left side of the stage, he counted five additional, rapid shots originating from the parking lot behind. Followed by no further shooting.

When they reached the parking lot, two men were down and two more stood over the bodies.

The chaos became choreographed as moves practiced during countless drills were automatically performed almost simultaneously as Danimal's base security took charge.

Weston was approached, triaged, and rushed into one waiting ambulance. Mrs. Weston was rushed to a second ambulance.

The chaplain's injuries were either fatal or minor, judging from the medics' lack of urgency when they reached him.

More security personnel arrived. Two men were confirmed dead.

Within minutes the entire base was locked down. The voice came on the speaker advising everyone to "shelter in place." Meaning hunker down until the situation was secured.

Otto and Gaspar hung back from the working professionals.

"We should go," Otto said, her attention focused on the crime scene. "Those two authorized FBI agents will be around somewhere, maybe calling backup. We can't be caught here."

Though Gaspar agreed, he told her to wait there a minute and slipped around the edges to reach Danimal, who was questioning Weston's bodyguards. The same bodyguards who'd failed to protect their boss. Danimal stepped aside to give Gaspar a brief account of the shooting according to the first witnesses.

"Looks like a lone shooter. That guy," he pointed to one of the two dead men. "No ID yet. He approached the back of the stage about halfway through the service as if he was authorized to be there. When Weston stood for the benediction, he pulled his pistol and shot Weston in the left shoulder, and both legs. Mrs. Weston was shot in the right femur. The other victim is one of Weston's bodyguards. These two guys say the shooter killed their buddy and then they killed him."

Gaspar reviewed the crime scene briefly, then nodded. "It could have happened that way," he said. "Where did they take Weston?"

"He requested Tampa Southern," Danimal said. "Call me later and I'll fill you in. I've got to get back to work."

"Thanks," Gaspar said, then approached the two bodies for a closer look.

The bodyguard lay face down, lifeless, unmoving in a lake of his own blood. Black hair. Bulky guy. Maybe six feet. Maybe 200 pounds of pumped-up shoulders and biceps. Big, but not big enough to stop bullets fired dead on target at close range.

Less than three feet away, the scrawny shooter was face up on the tarmac, one glassy eye still open and the other covered with a black patch. Like several others attending today's memorial, grotesque scars from a healed wound gouged his forehead. One cheek was sunken because half the upper jawbone had disappeared some time ago. His Army BDUs were well worn and oversized for the wasted body inside them. Boots polished but old and scuffed as if he'd had trouble lifting his feet to walk. His deformed right hand still gripped the FN Five-seven

240 | DIANE CAPRI

pistol he'd meant to use to get up close and execute his target.

Brain injuries manifested in unpredictable ways. It was possible the shooter had been unable to control his homicidal impulses and simply lashed out at the nearest targets, but the whole scene felt darkly, undeniably intentional to Gaspar. Shooting Weston in the back. Shooter knowing he'd die trying to kill. Hitting Weston three times before the two wild shots injured others nearby. A crowd of military families and personnel watching.

It felt very, very personal.

No question the shooter was a man with vengeance on his mind.

But he wasn't Jack Reacher.

Gaspar wondered if Reacher would experience a pang of regret for having his unfinished business with Weston finished for him by this damaged, deranged soldier.

After he'd absorbed all he could about the situation, Gaspar returned to Otto and said, "Let's go."

They slipped weapons back into place and merged with the audience as security herded them to their cars and eventually exited the base though the nearby Bayshore Gate.

While they waited in the long line of traffic, Gaspar told her about the glinting rifle barrel in the sniper's nest, the bodyguard, and the shooter.

"The shooter's definitely not Reacher?"

"Definitely not. Although it could have been him in the nest. Impossible to know."

Otto nodded, thinking. "So. Disabled veteran? Maybe served under Weston's supervision?"

"Iraq has been Weston's location for long enough. They could have crossed paths there, even if Weston wasn't the guy's

CO," Gaspar said. "The shooter was disabled, for sure. Likely a vet. But if we're betting, I'd say he was focused and lucid when he planned and executed this plan."

"Why?"

"Two reasons. First, logistics. Getting close enough to Weston to shoot him required stealth and cleverness, but also logic and planning. He had to get on base, locate the best shooting position, have a weapon, and a long list of other things. None of that could have been accomplished if he'd suffered from a significant mental deficiency."

Otto nodded, considering. "Maybe. One thing we know: the number of vets who suffered head injuries during both Iraq and Afghanistan is staggering. In earlier wars, they wouldn't have survived wounds like that. We can keep so many more alive now, but the treatments aren't great and definitely don't fix the damage."

Gaspar said nothing.

"Sometimes, they suffer strokes and seizures. Behavior can be erratic, even violent," Otto said, running through her internal list of possibles. "Maybe he had a grievance against Weston. And maybe he was just not rational. What's your second thing?"

"He pulled it off. He reached Weston, armed, on a military base designed to stop him. He shot five times before a private bodyguard took him out, but not before he mortally wounded the bodyguard. And he had physical disabilities beyond the head trauma. All of that says logic, planning, knowledge, focus." Gaspar took a deep breath. Discussions about the abilities of the injured and disabled were bound to lead somewhere he wasn't willing to go. "My money says the guy specifically planned to kill Weston and he was willing to die trying. But with nothing

242 | DIANE CAPRI

more to go on, it's impossible to know. And, more to the point, not our case. We've got our own problems. So now what?"

"Assuming Weston survives, those two FBI agents will execute his arrest warrant today, no matter what," Otto said. "Let's see if we can get any more out of him about Reacher before we lose the only good lead we've got."

"Okay. But what about Reacher?"

"What about him?"

"If he was the one in that sniper's nest, he knows Weston wasn't dead at the time he got into the ambulance. And he knows where to find Weston now."

"And he's at least thirty minutes ahead of us," Otto said.

Gaspar increased the sedan's speed to tailgate the car in front of them. Maybe today was the day to face Reacher after all. Get some answers right from the source. Finish this assignment and move on.

CHAPTER SEVEN

TAMPA SOUTHERN HOSPITAL WAS located about six miles from MacDill Air Force Base near the opposite end of Bayshore Boulevard. Gaspar stretched out as he settled into the oversized seat and drove along perhaps one of the most beautiful stretches of pavement in Florida.

Immediately outside the Bayshore Gate they passed residential property on the west side of the winding two-lane. At the first traffic light, Interbay Boulevard, more than half the traffic turned west.

Gaspar continued through the residential section, past the streets that led to the Tampa Yacht Club entrances on the right, past Ballast Point. After the next traffic light at Gandy Boulevard, the two lanes separated into a wide divided linear park that ran along the entire shoreline of Hillsborough Bay toward downtown.

Otto seemed to enjoy the scenery, too. As they passed Plant Key Bridge, she said, "I've never been to Tampa before. What's that little island out there?"

"It's called Plant Key. Privately owned. It was originally built by a railroad baron named Henry Plant."

"He built an island?"

"Well, the Army Corps of Engineers dredged the bay and piled up the dirt, but Plant did the rest. That Moorish looking building was his home, called Minaret. Maybe built in the 1890's. Plant was constructing the Tampa Bay Hotel, now the University of Tampa. He was competing with Henry Flagler for the rich and famous vacationers of the time."

"Don't try to tell me about competition, Chico," Otto said. "I'm from Detroit, where the weak are killed and eaten. There've never been rivals bloodthirstier than the Fords and the Dodge brothers."

He laughed. "Now, there's a great restaurant out there called George's Place. If we get a chance, we'll have dinner there. The chef is amazing."

Otto glanced toward him and smiled for the first time today. "You mean we'd eat something that doesn't come out of a ptomaine cart? What a sweet-talker you are."

He felt a grin sneak up on his lips and some of the unrelenting tension released. "Stick with me, Susie Wong. You ain't seen nothin' yet. You've never tried a gold brick sundae, I'll bet."

When she laughed like that, she seemed younger and prettier, Gaspar realized. She was so serious most of the time that he'd never noticed that about her. She was young. She could still have a normal life with a family. He wondered if she ever thought about that.

"The homes along here across from the waterfront are amazing, too. I've stayed in hotels smaller than that one," she said, pointing to an 8,000-square-foot Georgian-style mansion.

"Reminds me of a similar stretch along Lake St. Claire. In Grosse Pointe, just outside Detroit. I drive out there on weekends sometimes in the summer. Beautiful."

She sounded homesick. Interesting, Gaspar thought. Until now, she'd never seemed to care that she wasn't on her way back for Thanksgiving.

There was no further landmass in Hillsborough Bay until they reached the bridge to Florida Key where Tampa Southern Hospital was located. Gaspar merged onto the bridge and crossed the water before entering the driveway between the hospital and the parking garage.

"Drop me off at the entrance and park the car, okay?" Otto said. "I'll find out what's going on and meet you inside."

"You got it, Susie Wong," he replied. She left the car and he watched her sign in at the information desk and head toward the elevators before he drove to the garage alone.

CHAPTER EIGHT

FOUR PEOPLE OCCUPIED THE small waiting room when Gaspar arrived upstairs. Two men he'd never seen before. Two women he recognized. The men sat a few chairs apart and directly across from the wall-mounted television tuned to a football game. If they noticed or cared about his arrival, they didn't betray themselves.

He was relieved to see both women look up when he entered, which meant he hadn't become invisible since they'd seen him last.

Jess Kimball, the *Taboo* reporter, sat closer to the entrance, as if to ensure she'd be the first to pounce when worthy prey arrived. There was something about her that suggested barely contained anger. Given her feelings about Weston, maybe she was annoyed that the shooter had failed. She was intense, which made Gaspar want to know her story. She was young to be so driven. Usually that kind of idealism came from tragedy and betrayal, in Gaspar's experience. Which was what he figured had happened to her. But what?

The other woman was Jennifer Lane, Samantha Weston's

lawyer. She sat in the corner across from the entry door where she had a clear view of the entire room and its occupants. Gaspar knew a lot of lawyers, but none that were Velcroed to their clients like this one. What was going on there?

He shrugged. Both women were too young to have known Reacher during the Weston murder investigation, which made them vaguely interesting, but irrelevant to his mission.

He absorbed the rest of the scene in a quick glance. One wall of the waiting room featured large plate glass windows overlooking the water. The opposite wall sported a small opening filled with a sliding frosted glass panel behind which, presumably, someone was working. Otto was probably chatting that someone up now. Which was great, because it meant he didn't have to do it.

Gaspar settled into one of the molded plastic chairs, extended his legs, folded his hands over his flat stomach and closed his eyes. The others might think he was sleeping. If nothing interesting happened within five minutes, he would be.

Three minutes later, Otto came in and sat next to him. "I spoke with the Westons' assigned nurse. His name is Steve Kent. He served at MacDill, so he has the necessary clearances, he said. He was also a Navy medic for a while, and respected Weston's service in Iraq. That's why he requested the duty."

"Since when do you need a security clearance to be a civilian nurse to a retired officer?" Gaspar asked without opening his eyes.

"Probably depends on the officer," Otto said. "Anyway, I told him we had a plane to catch and he said he'd take us in as soon as Weston can answer questions."

"Okay," he replied, closing his eyes again. "Did he say anything else I need to know right now?"

Gaspar heard her sigh and imagined she was rolling her eyes, knowing full well what he was up to. Unlike Gaspar, Otto had never been a soldier. She hadn't developed the habit of resting when she could. She got up and left him to it.

When he checked through his lashes, he saw her pacing the room, stopping now and again to glance out the window at Bayshore Boulevard. On a clear day, Gaspar knew she could have seen Plant Key and George's Place and probably all the way to MacDill at the opposite end of the linear park. Not today. Heavy clouds had moved in, bringing congested air that obscured the sightline. He settled his eyes truly shut.

Gaspar figured even if Reacher was in the vicinity, he couldn't reach Weston as long as Weston was still in surgery. Gaspar might have dropped off for a quick twenty winks, but he heard Otto engage in subdued conversation with one of the women. Probably Kimball. Reporters were chatty by nature. Probably not Lane. Lawyers were notoriously tight-lipped. Trying to talk to Lane would be a waste of time. Whatever Otto found out from whoever she was talking to, she'd tell him eventually. He let his breathing flatten and even out as he felt himself dropping again toward sleep.

He was almost there when the door opened and Gaspar raised his eyelids enough to see a woman dressed in pink surgical scrubs enter. "You're the FBI agents?" she asked.

"That's right," Otto said, directing her to the seat next to Gaspar and leaving Kimball and Lane behind her looking miffed at being excluded.

"I'm Trista Blanke, O.R. Patient Coordinator," she said. "I've been told I should give you an update on Mr. and Mrs. Weston. They should both be out of surgery shortly. Mr. Weston's most serious wound was the shot to the back of his shoulder. The bullet traveled through his body, which is better than most alternatives. But it nicked an artery. He lost a lot of blood and the repair surgery lasted a bit longer than it otherwise would have."

"And Mrs. Weston?" Otto asked.

"She was wounded in the right thigh. Again, the bullet traveled through, but it shattered the femur. She should be fine once reconstruction is completed," she said. "They'll be in recovery for an hour or so after the procedures."

"When can we talk to them?" Otto asked.

"When they're out of surgery, you can give it a try. But until the anesthesia wears off, they may not make much sense."

"Thanks," Otto said.

"No problem," she said before she approached Jennifer Lane, likely to deliver the same news. Kimball crowded in to hear.

"We are probably wasting our time," Otto said, quietly.

Gaspar didn't argue. Except for the possibility of running into Reacher, he figured their time could be much better spent eating. He settled back into his waiting posture and reclosed his eyes, hoping for a quiet five minutes.

When Ms. Blanke had completed her mission and advanced toward the exit, Gaspar heard Otto join her, asking, "Where can I get a cup of coffee?"

Four minutes, forty-five seconds later, the football game ended and the two guys who'd been watching left the room. Gaspar was now alone with the two women. In his bachelor days, he'd have considered that a fringe benefit of the job.

Jessica Kimball spoke first. "Are you planning to arrest both Westons when they come out of recovery?"

"What reason do you have for arresting Samantha Weston?" Jennifer Lane demanded.

Kimball replied, "He's FBI. The Asian woman, too. Why else would they be here?"

"Is that true?" Lane asked.

Gaspar's eyes remained closed and he said nothing. Otto would have bristled at the assumption she was Asian. Oh, sure, she looked like her Vietnamese mother. But she considered herself 100% tall, blonde, sturdy, stubborn German, like her father. Gaspar grinned and said nothing.

Kimball walked over and kicked the sole of his right shoe. Not hard. Just enough to jostle a normal person to attention. But the strike sent painful shock waves up his right leg and into his right side where the muscles had collapsed and the nerves touched things they weren't meant to touch.

"You're not sleeping," Kimball said.

"Checking my eyelids for holes," he replied, willing his pain to settle down. Which never worked. Biofeedback was bunk. Maybe pain was in the brain, but despite his exercise of will, his leg settled into the dull thumping he'd long ago accepted as normal. He opened his eyes, but didn't alter his posture. "What can I do for you, Ms. Kimball?"

"Same thing the FBI has been doing for me for a decade," Kimball said, bitterly. "Nothing."

Lane cut in belligerently. "Do you have an arrest warrant for Samantha Weston? You intend to arrest her while she's incapacitated and unable to understand her rights, Agent Gaspar?"

"Obviously, she understands she has a right to an attorney, since you're here," Gaspar replied without moving. "The only way your presence here makes any sense to me is that she's been expecting us. Which means someone tipped her off. When I find out who did the tipping, you may have yourself another client."

The expression on Lane's face suggested he'd hit the bulls-eye. Most leaks were intentional. If someone had warned Samantha Weston of her impending arrest, the notice was tactical. Which made him wonder briefly, as a matter of professional curiosity, what the local agents were really up to with Weston. If they already had a warrant supported by probable cause for arrest, why did they want his wife?

"Maybe I don't need your client, Ms. Lane. I'm only interested in the original murder investigation," Gaspar said. "What do you know about that?"

"Samantha wasn't living in Tampa back then," Jennifer Lane replied. "Nor was I."

Kimball said, "I've investigated thoroughly for *Taboo*, and I was at the gunman's execution. So I probably know more than she does."

The waiting room door opened again and Otto entered with four cups of black coffee. Everyone took a cup and spent a few moments adding and stirring.

Lane sipped and swallowed before she asked, "Are you thinking today's shooting is somehow about that old case?"

"What do you think?" Gaspar replied.

"I doubt it," Otto said. "Seventeen years is a long time for any normal person to carry a grudge."

Like a woman with personal experience, Kimball said, "Not where your kids are concerned, it isn't."

"Say you're right," Lane said to her. "What do you think is going on here?"

Jennifer Lane looked young and inexperienced. How'd she get a powerhouse client like Weston's wife? Curious situation, at the very least, Gaspar thought again.

Jess Kimball was about the same age as Lane, but she

seemed more worldly somehow. As if she'd been through tough times that had aged her and forged her titanium spine. She said, "We need to know how today's shooter is connected to Weston. It wasn't a random shooting, because the guy went right up to Weston and fired only at him. When we get the name of the shooter, I should be able to tell you what's going on."

"What makes you so sure?" Otto asked.

"I do very thorough research, Agent Otto. If Weston's sneezed in the wrong direction, I've found out about it," Kimball said, clearly miffed at the perceived slight to her reporting skills. "Listen: this guy is a miserable human being who's caused nothing but heartache wherever he's gone. This wasn't the first time someone has tried to erase Weston from the planet. He's had more lives than an alley cat already. Sorting through the list of people waiting in line for a chance to kill him will take some time."

Before Otto had a chance to reply, the waiting room door opened again. Every time it happened, Gaspar tensed a bit. Expecting Reacher. But so far, he hadn't materialized.

This time, four people entered ahead of a short, stout man dressed in hospital scrubs. The smallish waiting room was instantly overcrowded.

Gaspar recognized the two FBI agents he'd seen at the memorial service intending to arrest Weston for a laundry list of crimes against the government. Lane and Kimball weren't too far off in their assessment of the FBI's intentions, though they had been led a bit astray regarding the identity of the Bureau's official team for the arrest.

There was an awkward moment while everyone seemed blinded by the unexpected presence of the others before the stout man in scrubs began threading his way through the group on his way to the interior door. One of the agents stopped his progress by pulling out his badge wallet. "I'm Special Agent Edward Crane and this is Special Agent Derek Bartos." Crane, Gaspar thought. He knew—and didn't much like—the man. "We're here to take recorded statements from Thomas Weston and his wife, Samantha Weston." Crane pointed toward one of the other two newcomers, a tall redhead wearing jeans and blazer over a white tee-shirt and a pixie hair cut suitable for a woman ten years younger. "This is Judge Willa Carson and her court reporter, Ms. Natalie Chernow."

Gaspar's right eyebrow shot up. There weren't that many Federal judges in Florida and he'd met most of them several times—the FBI and the federal bench routinely worked cooperatively. Judge Carson's jurisdiction was the Middle District of Florida, though, and Gaspar generally stayed in his own sandbox in the Southern District, so he'd never met her.

But he'd heard stories about the freewheeling Willa Carson, who was said to care less for precedent and statutes than her own version of appropriate justice. Some said Carson's conduct was unjudicial. Others said she was a breath of fresh air. All of which, for a law-and-order man like Gaspar, wasn't usually good news. But he'd mellowed lately on the rule-following. He could hardly fault Judge Carson for doing the same.

The stout man spoke up. "I'm Steven Kent, physician's assistant assigned to both patients. Colonel Weston is out of surgery and stable, though he's too groggy to answer questions yet. He'll be moved in about thirty minutes." His tone was not exactly disrespectful, but he wasn't deferential, either. "Mrs. Weston should be moved by then as well. I'll let you know."

Kent turned smartly like a soldier on parade and left without further comment. Brief silence reigned.

Otto stood and introduced herself and Gaspar to the new arrivals before she said, "There's a coffee pot at the station across the hall. Anybody interested?"

Jennifer Lane held out her empty cup and said, "I'd love another one. Would you mind? I'd come with you, but I need to watch these new guys."

Bad move. She'd insulted the FBI, which raised Otto's hackles along with those of the other agents. Gaspar remained unruffled. Lawyers were always sanctimonious, in his experience. Being a lawyer herself, Otto couldn't very well say so. Gaspar hid his grin as she grudgingly collected Lane's cup.

"I'm fine," Kimball replied.

"Judge Carson? Coffee?" Otto offered.

Carson moved to join her, towering over Otto and glancing back as they headed for the door. "Surely you people can play nice until I get back. If not," she looked Gaspar in the eye, "go ahead and shoot them all."

Gaspar laughed out loud. Yep. Judge Willa Carson might be worth the drive up from Miami on the right case. He'd keep the idea in mind. If he ever got back to his normal job.

CHAPTER NINE

AFTER THE DOOR CLOSED behind Otto and the Judge, Crane said, "Agent Gaspar, can I have a word with you outside, please?"

Gaspar stood, stretched, ignored the pain and forced himself not to limp as he followed Crane into the corridor. When they reached the window at the end of the hallway where they were unlikely to be overheard, Crane asked, "What are you doing here, Gaspar?"

"Enjoying the sunshine."

"Still the same smart ass."

"I think you mentioned that the last time our paths crossed, Crane."

"When I saw you at the memorial, I called in. Miami doesn't know why you're here. Have you gone rogue, Gaspar?"

"Possibly," he replied.

"If you're connected to Weston, you're going down. Got that?"

Gaspar ignored the threat, which was par for the course with Crane. "Rumor says you've got a warrant in your pocket.

Brought along the judge herself, just to cover your bases. The bad news, though: you arrest Weston, you won't need a court reporter. He's not talking to you until he gets a lawyer, and probably not then."

"He's got a lawyer, and he'll talk."

"Lane says she's the wife's lawyer. Not his," Gaspar said.

"Not to me, she didn't." If he jutted his chin any farther, he might fall over from the weight of his fat head.

"You're thinking Weston's going to confess to something? Have you ever talked to the guy? He wouldn't tell you how he takes his coffee unless he had a damn good reason."

"He must have a good reason, then."

Gaspar hadn't considered that Weston would confess. He mulled this over, pushed the idea this way and that, like kneading bread. Couldn't make it work.

"What reason?"

"Don't know. Don't care." Crane sounded like a guy grunting his way through the defensive line. "He's committed about a hundred counts of treason. Murder. Grand larceny. You name it. The guy's a scum-bucket. I get it on the record in front of a Federal judge before he croaks, that's all I care about."

"You think Weston is dying? You're planning a dying declaration?" Gaspar laughed a good two seconds before he controlled himself. "He was winged. Two busted legs and a messed up shoulder. That's it. He's not dying. You're wasting your time."

"Wise up. He's got cancer. He'll be dead by the end of the month. It's his wife he's worried about protecting now. He thinks we'll charge her with his crimes."

"Why would he think that?"

Crane shrugged and made no reply. Which was all the reply Gaspar needed. Crane must have threatened to charge Weston's wife. And Weston must have believed the threat. Nothing else would puff Crane's confidence up so far.

Steven Kent came around the corner and saw them standing at the end of the hallway. "You can come in now," he said, then stuck his head into the waiting room and made the same announcement to the others.

"What about Weston's wife?" Gaspar pressed.

"That's his motivation. He's trying to save her ass," Crane said.

Gaspar wondered whether the wife cared that much about Weston, since she'd filed for divorce. He shrugged. "Will it work?"

"Depends on what he says, doesn't it?" Crane strode away from Gaspar like a man who'd spiked the ball in the end zone.

CHAPTER TEN

THEY CROWDED AROUND WESTON'S hospital bed in a large, open recovery room that had been cleared of all patients except Weston and his wife. She was obviously still out cold, but Weston was at least approaching consciousness—quietly moaning, eyelids fluttering. A blanket covered him from the waist down, obscuring the state of reconstruction done to both legs. His shoulder was bandaged, but not casted. Gaspar guessed the repairs were done on the inside.

Unless he perked up pretty markedly, they weren't going to get much of a statement from him. And even if they did and he said something worthwhile, it wouldn't carry much weight later, given the amount of drugs in his system. Undeterred, Natalie Chernow, the court reporter, had set up her machine near the head of the bed to be sure she accurately heard and recorded anything he might babble. She also activated a tape recorder. Belt and suspenders, Gaspar supposed.

Judge Carson stood at the foot of the bed, the better to see and hear everything as it happened, should anything happen.

Lane said she would act as Weston's representative for the

purpose of the statement so they didn't have to call in another lawyer, which wasn't exactly kosher. But nothing about the situation was normal and it wasn't Gaspar's case, so he wasn't going to object. Even though he'd like to whip that "I told you so" smirk off Crane's face.

Lane stood next to the court reporter, Crane and his crony Bartos stood across the bed from Gaspar and Otto, and Kimball pressed herself into position beside them.

"Wait," Lane said to her. "What the hell are you doing in here?"

"First Amendment and Florida's Sunshine law. Press would be allowed in a courtroom for the statement," Kimball pointed out, "so I can't be excluded just because proceedings are in a hospital."

Lane appealed to Judge Carson, who ruled that Kimball could stay. Gaspar and Otto, too. Carson offered no explanation for her ruling.

Gaspar didn't expect to learn much, especially since Weston had so far only managed the occasional groan, though it made sense to play things out just in case he got chatty. You never knew. It was just barely possible he might cough up a lead on Reacher that he and Otto could follow up later. Mainly they stayed because it would have looked odd to leave at that point.

And then Weston opened his eyes. When he saw Gaspar, his mouth opened in a wide, drugged, silly smile. His pupils were dilated and his speech slurred when he gleefully asked, "Did my guys get him?"

"What?" Otto asked, leaning in.

Weston's voice was weak, whispery, hard to hear. But unmistakably cheerful. "Reacher. Shot me. Did my guys kill him? Is he dead?"

Otto asked, "You lured Reacher to the memorial so your bodyguards could kill him?"

Crane glared at Otto, but she didn't see him. Crane spoke up. "Colonel Weston, the shooter was Michael Vernon. He was killed at the scene. You knew him, right? He served under you in Iraq for two years. Hit by an IED, remember? Two buddies died. Vernon survived. Blamed you for the whole thing, would be my guess."

Weston sank into his pillows and closed his eyes again. His breathing became more ragged. Steven Kent must have noticed something irregular on the monitors because he came into the room and checked the machines.

"Ten minutes. No more," he said to Crane. "Otherwise, he won't survive the night."

"You said his injuries weren't life threatening," Crane said.

Kent stood his ground, "I said normally not life threatening. We need to keep it that way, don't you think?"

Crane didn't like it, but he backed off. Gaspar figured Crane's restraint wouldn't last long.

But it was true that Weston looked bad. When he found out his plan to kill Reacher failed, his fragile strength seemed to evaporate. Gaspar wondered how many times Weston's vendetta against Reacher had failed before. Weston's reach was extensive, inside the government and out. Another possible explanation for Reacher's hiding so far off the grid that not even a bloodhound could find him. At least until Reacher could take care of Weston or something else got Weston first. Which didn't seem so paranoid right at the moment.

The court reporter announced she was ready.

Judge Carson started the proceedings by opening the record and covering all the legal necessities. She said she'd granted an emergency motion for a recorded statement from Mr. and Mrs. Weston because the FBI represented to her that the statement was essential to an ongoing criminal investigation likely to be harmed if Mr. and Mrs. Weston became incapacitated.

And because Weston's counsel consented.

Jennifer Lane made a short statement about the limited nature of her legal representation and her clients' consent. Observers said nothing.

Finally, Crane began his questions. He could have spent the ten minutes he'd been allotted following up on Weston's plan to kill Reacher, which was the only thing Gaspar was interested in hearing about, but instead his questions focused on Weston's private security company operating in Iraq. Each question was accusatory and belligerent, Gaspar thought. Maybe a little desperate. But it didn't matter. Crane was destined to get nowhere.

Weston had exhausted his available energy on Reacher. Now, he was mostly non-responsive. He grunted a couple of times to signal yes or no. He moaned. He seemed to be almost unconscious. Ms. Chernow's transcript would be mostly a list of questions followed by empty spaces.

After the promised ten minutes, Steven Kent returned to check his patient. "I'm sorry, but that's it. Colonel Weston isn't able to continue."

Crane's annoyance was on full display. "But we're not finished."

Kent replied, "For now you are. You can come back in a couple hours and try again if you want. Or you can call me if you don't want to make an unnecessary trip."

Crane opened his mouth to argue again, but Judge Carson said, "Thank you, Mr. Kent. We'll close the record at this time and resume later this evening or as soon as Colonel Weston is capable."

Crane said, "Let's question Mrs. Weston now, then."

Samantha Weston was in the room's only remaining bed. A curtain separated her bed from her husband's. Kent pulled the curtain back and checked her health indicators. He shook his head. "Mrs. Weston is still sedated. She's not able to communicate at this time, either, I'm afraid."

Crane's mouth was set in a hard line. Gaspar watched him fight to control his anger. He was a pouter, this guy. Too soft. When he didn't get his way, he was whinier than Gaspar's ten-year-old daughter. The thought made Gaspar smile and Crane glared back as if he might start a fistfight. Gaspar struggled not to laugh. He caught Otto's eye and saw her reaction was the same as his.

Judge Carson saw the lay of the land. She did what judges do. She wrapped it up. "Is there anything else anyone wants to put on the record at this time?"

No one raised anything. She closed the record and everyone left the room except Ms. Chernow, who stayed to pack up her equipment.

In the corridor, Crane seized the initiative again. "Judge, we'd like to continue in two hours. We're worried that these witnesses won't survive the night. If they don't, our case will be irreparably harmed—"

Judge Carson headed him off before he could get too amped up. "Fine. Ms. Chernow exists on nuts and dried fruit she carries in her purse. On that diet, I'd be dead in a week, and I'm hungry. Anyone want to join me for dinner at George's Place? No need to change clothes. We can grab a quick bite in the Sunset Bar."

Because refusing a dinner invitation from the judge on your

case wasn't a smart move, everyone officially interested in Weston should have accepted.

But Crane said, "I need to review my file to streamline my questions. I'll just grab something from a vending machine."

Agent Bartos, probably figuring it would be a bad career move to contradict his boss, pulled out his wallet and left for the nearest sandwich.

Jennifer Lane seemed torn by indecision. If she stayed, she could keep an eye on Agents Crane and Bartos, but she'd have to stop watching Gaspar and Otto. Not to mention ticking off the Judge on her case. If she went to dinner, though, Crane and Bartos would remain unsupervised and who knows what mischief they'd get up to without her to restrain them.

Gaspar stifled his smirk and glanced over toward Otto, who pretended to yawn, probably to cover amusement.

"I'm in," Jess Kimball announced.

Otto said, "Me, too." Who knew why? Her motives were usually a mystery to Gaspar.

No mystery at all regarding Gaspar's motivation for accepting Judge Carson's invitation. She'd offered to buy and he was hungry. Simple as that.

CHAPTER ELEVEN

JUDGE CARSON'S MERCEDES CLK convertible zipped along Bayshore Boulevard like a homing pigeon on its return flight. Jessica Kimball's SUV followed. Gaspar brought up the rear in the rented sedan.

George's Place was the only five-star restaurant in South Tampa, as far as Gaspar knew. He'd never eaten at another one. Which might not mean anything. He didn't come to Tampa often and he wasn't a big foodie. A good Cuban sandwich was good enough for him. And any dessert made with guava.

The effortless drive from Tampa Southern to the Plant Key location was as beautiful tonight as it had been earlier in the day. Bayshore Boulevard beribboned the water's edge along the miles in both directions. The full moon and lighted balustrade created a warm, magical picture his daughters always loved.

"How about a quick recap?" Otto asked, as if she were actually giving him an option.

"Sure."

She ticked off her conclusions raising one finger at a time as if they were facts. Which they probably were. "Weston put the word out and staged his attendance at this memorial because he wanted to lure Reacher. He believed Reacher would try to kill him. He made himself a human target. Then his bodyguards would kill Reacher. His purpose was to exact revenge on Reacher."

Gaspar didn't argue. Suicide by cop. Maybe a bit pedestrian for a Machiavelli like Weston, but not a rare motive among those angry and feeling persecuted by law enforcement.

"Weston planned to kill Reacher for sixteen years. Don't you think that's bizarre?" she asked.

"I do." No real reason to argue. Cold revenge and all that. Besides, he was hungry and didn't want to prolong the discussion. He rolled the window down, got a good whiff of the exposed plankton at low tide, and promptly filled the hole with glass again.

Otto's speculation started next.

"The Boss knew of Weston's plan and thought it might work," she said. "He knew Reacher could show up. The memorial was well publicized. Reacher might have learned about it, depending on where the hell he's hiding at the moment. The Boss knew we could get caught in the crossfire."

Gaspar shrugged. "Probably."

"You don't care?" she asked, pugnaciously as usual.

He could feel her anguish, but none of his own. He had no illusions about their Boss. This assignment had almost killed them both more than once already. Why should today be different?

"Doesn't matter whether I care or not, Sunshine."

Her shoulders slumped as her steely defiance melted. "He knew, and sent us in anyway," she said. "That's the worst part."

"It is what it is. You know that. Stop expecting him to

change." Gaspar had twenty years to go and no alternative career he could fathom. But Otto was ambitious. She had plans. Options. She should move on before this assignment got her killed or ruined her life, whichever came first. She should have moved on already. But he knew she wouldn't. So he said nothing more.

After a couple of seconds of silence emphasizing Otto's malaise passed between them, she asked, "Did you see Reacher anywhere?"

Gaspar remembered the glint in the sniper's nest, but wagged his head. "Weston's delusional. So's the Boss."

She seemed to feel slightly better when he voiced what amounted to confirmation that Otto hadn't been derelict somehow and missed Reacher when he was right there, larger than life.

Gaspar said, "Our flight's at midnight. We've got maybe four hours left to kill before we're stuck here. We can have a decent dinner, find out what that reporter knows about Reacher, go back to the hospital for Weston's statement, and then head out."

When she didn't reply, he said, "You're such a foodie. I figured you'd be thrilled about our dining experience, Susie Wong. You're in for a treat."

"It's about time you took me to a decent joint, Chico," she replied, a small grin lifting the corners of her lips.

Which was also true. So Gaspar laughed and he felt good when she joined in, for once.

CHAPTER TWELVE

BEFORE THE TRAFFIC LIGHT at the intersection of Bayshore and Gandy Boulevard, Carson's convertible pulled into the left turn lane and stopped briefly before crossing the eastbound traffic lanes to reach the Plant Key Bridge. A simple two-lane track lying flat above the shallow Hillsborough Bay. One way on and one way off the private island. Which was probably both the good news and the bad news, depending on the traffic and whether one was inclined to feel trapped.

Carson rushed into the surprisingly crowded parking lot at the front entrance.

The red brick building fairly twinkled in the gathering dark. Indoor lighting spilled cheerfully through the windows. The rest of the place was bathed by floodlights around the perimeter. Smaller light streams punctuated the darkness and the steel minaret on the roof.

Gaspar lost track of Carson and Kimball while he searched for an open parking space.

"This place is amazing," Otto said.

"What? Doesn't your Michigan house look exactly like that?"

"I thought it looked familiar," she said, which made him feel better. She'd emerged from her mood, at least.

"First time I came here," he said, "I was told the place was built as a private home. Can you imagine living in a place like this? Servants and horses and such, of course."

"Pretty idyllic setting for a restaurant, too," she replied, still taking everything in. "Now I really feel underdressed."

By the time he settled the sedan appropriately, Carson and Kimball must have already entered the building. Gaspar stopped to stretch when he got out of the sedan, like always. He acted like he was just being lazy. But the truth was that if he didn't stretch out his right leg, he'd fall flat on his face when he tried to move.

Otto watched and waited. "Kimball says she knows everything about the murder of Weston's family. Since Reacher was the investigating officer at the time, she may have some Intel or maybe a couple of leads helpful to us. Let's be sure we don't leave here without it, okay?"

"I'm driving. Can't drink. So I won't have anything better to do," Gaspar said and then set off at as quick a pace as he could manage. But Otto kept up easily. Which was how he judged himself and knew he was moving at glacial speed.

CHAPTER THIRTEEN

KIMBALL WAS WAITING AT the hostess station inside the front entrance. "Judge Carson said she'd be right back and we should look for a booth in the Sunset Bar."

"Lead the way," Gaspar said. He'd been inside the building before, but its old-world charm was no less impressive this time. Spanish influence was heavy, dark, massive, and spacious. He imagined gaslights and servants roaming the halls. Maybe his ancestors had served in such a place in Cuba.

The Sunset Bar was a much more casual eatery than Gaspar expected. A television, booths, a well-stocked bar that hugged the entire side of the room opposite the west-facing windows. Gaspar imagined magnificent sunsets could be enjoyed nightly.

Against all odds, there was one empty booth. The bad news: it was surrounded by listening ears and watching eyes. Which meant less opportunity for intelligence-gathering than Gaspar had hoped.

Kimball slid across the bench and Gaspar settled in next to her on the outside so he would have more room to stretch his right leg unobtrusively. Otto probably noticed. She noticed everything. She slid across the bench on the opposite side facing Kimball and leaving room for Carson opposite Gaspar.

Kimball leaned in and said quietly, "Those two guys over there?" She tilted her head to her right, indicating which ones she meant. "They get around. I saw them at the memorial service today. I noticed because they were also at the execution of the killer of Weston's family. A third guy was with them both times."

Impressive memory, Gaspar thought. Probably came in handy for a reporter.

Both men were Weston's age. Latin. Heavy-set. Casually and expensively dressed. They didn't look exactly like mobsters, but they weren't ordinary businessmen having an after work drink, either.

Otto was sitting upright now. In a conversational tone, she asked, "Do you know who they are?"

"That's one of the things on my list to find out."

"What did the third guy look like?" Gaspar asked, although he suspected he already knew.

"Like he'd been to hell and didn't make it back. What you'd notice about him first was a black eye patch covering an empty eye socket. Scars from a healed head injury." She hesitated a second. "Something wrong with one of his hands, too, but I didn't see it well enough to describe."

"That sounds like the fellow who shot Weston this morning. What did Crane say his name was?" Gaspar searched his memory for the name but before it came up, Otto supplied it.

"Michael Vernon."

Kimball nodded slowly as if she was searching her internal hard drive for data on Vernon and coming up empty. Which Gaspar figured was a ruse of some sort. Surely she'd found a way to get a look at the shooter earlier today. If so, she'd have already made this connection. Not that she owed him anything, but what other information was she holding back?

A waiter appeared at the table with menus and took drink orders. All three ordered coffee. Kimball and Otto ordered black. Gaspar requested *café con leche*, the rich, Cuban coffee heavily laced with heated milk.

"What's the best dinner on the menu?" Otto asked.

"You can't go wrong," the waiter replied. "George's Place has the best chefs in the city. The food here in the Sunset Bar is the same you'd get in the dining room."

Otto said, "What did you have for dinner?"

He grinned. "My favorite is the Thomas Jefferson Roast Beef. Hands down."

"I'll have that," Otto said, handing the menu back.

"I'd add the pear salad with gorgonzola," he said.

"Sold."

"Make it two," Kimball said.

"Three," Gaspar said.

"You got it," the waiter replied, before collecting their menus. "Be right back with the coffee while you wait."

When they were alone again, Kimball said, "Like you, I'm handicapped a bit because I don't know Tampa all that well. We can ask Judge Carson who those guys are. She might know, if they're regulars. Or if she doesn't, she can find out, since her husband owns the place."

Otto's eyes popped open a little wider, but Kimball had been watching her quarry and didn't notice.

Gaspar played white knight for Otto and pupil for Kimball at the same time. "I didn't know Carson's husband owned this restaurant. His name must be George?"

Kimball returned her gaze to Gaspar and Otto and her lips turned up in the most natural grin Gaspar had seen from her yet. She had a pretty face when she wasn't scowling. Which had been rarely so far.

"Let's give the Cuban dude a cigar," she said. "Speaking of which, Willa Carson smokes Cuban cigars. You probably didn't know that, either, did you?"

This time, Gaspar did laugh out loud. The flamboyant Judge Willa Carson was becoming more and more interesting. Too bad he wasn't posted to the FBI's Tampa field office. Sounded like a lot more fun than Miami.

"I'll be sure to ask her if she'd like an after-dinner smoke if we have the time." Cuban cigars were illegal, but the tobacco was now being grown in places like the Dominican Republic. The best ones were hand-rolled, of course, and aged until just the right flavor was to be experienced. Gaspar hadn't enjoyed a quality cigar since he left Miami and he missed them.

He'd have asked more questions, but Otto interrupted the foolishness. "So those two guys and the shooter killed today must be locals. These two must also know Weston. Might have known the Weston family shooter, too, if they got permission to attend his execution."

Kimball said, "Makes sense to me."

"So whatever connection all five men have must relate back in time, at least, to the murder of Weston's family," Otto continued.

If you didn't know her, you'd think she was simply musing out loud. But she'd already reached conclusions and was just polishing them.

Gaspar said nothing.

"Makes sense," Kimball replied. "I can't confirm that, based on my investigation so far, but it's a good working hypothesis and probably true. You're FBI agents. You could ask them. It's illegal to lie to a federal agent."

"You said Weston owed money to a gang that he didn't pay," Otto said. "You said that's why his family was killed."

"Yes."

"What kind of gang? Drugs? Human trafficking?"

Kimball shook her head. "The gang itself was probably involved in all of that. But Weston's vice was gambling. Got in way over his head, as gamblers often do."

"Back then, when Weston's family was murdered, gambling was mostly illegal here except for Greyhound racing," Gaspar supplied for Otto's benefit.

"Dog racing?" Otto said. "There's that much money involved in dog racing?"

"I guess there could be," Kimball said. "But Weston's gambling was the illegal kind. The allegations that Reacher investigated at the time involved pari-mutuel betting."

"OTB," Gaspar explained. "Off track betting. Down in the Miami office, we've got several OTB joints on our constant watch list. It's legal and regulated these days. In Florida, OTB is a money maker for the state. But it's also a cesspool of corruption where a guy with a gambling problem can get into really big trouble."

"Exactly. Weston got in way over his head. He was employed by Uncle Sam in a military job that, well, let's just say it didn't pay a million a year."

"He owed a million bucks?" Gaspar asked.

Kimball nodded. "He had no way to come up with that kind of money. He was a high-profile guy here and the gang decided to make an example of him. They told him to pay up or his family would pay for him. Apparently, he chose option two. Scumbag."

Kimball stopped talking while the waiter delivered the coffee.

When he left, Otto said, "You're saying Reacher discovered all of that and arrested Weston, but the locals couldn't prove any of it? So Weston walked away?"

Gaspar thought that sounded exactly like Reacher's methods. He'd have figured everything out and handled the matter himself. He didn't worry much about whether the courts accepted his proof.

Kimball sipped her coffee and returned Otto's level gaze. "That's how it looks from the file and everything else I've found. Weston didn't pull the trigger, but he didn't do anything to stop the killing, either. Of course he denied all involvement. He had an alibi. The shooter confessed. There was no evidence of Weston's debt. No evidence that the threat had been made by the gang or ignored by Weston. The gang leader certainly didn't come forward."

"No admissible evidence against Weston, so he was released. And Reacher was already gone by the time everything was sorted out."

As Otto completed her sentence, the fourth member of their dinner party arrived and slid into the booth across from Gaspar.

"From Weston's questions at the hospital, I gather your assignment has something to do with Jack Reacher," Carson said as she waved to the waiter to let him know we were all collected. Seeing they were drinking coffee, she ordered *café con leche* for herself and picked up the menu for a quick look. Gaspar figured she had to have it memorized by now. "I met him once when he was here."

"You met who?" Otto asked.

"Who was here?" Kimball asked simultaneously.

Carson decided on dinner, put the menu down, and glanced at Otto and Kimball. "Jack Reacher. He didn't stay long. But I'm told he never does."

The waiter took her order and refilled the coffee. He was even more attentive now that the boss's wife was in the house.

"What was Reacher doing here?" Otto asked, after the waiter left.

Carson settled back into the booth and turned slightly so she was facing everyone. She seemed to make a few quick decisions before she answered. "This is not my case. If it were, I wouldn't be discussing this with you. I'm on call tonight and that's the only reason I agreed to preside over the two sworn statements."

Gaspar figured she was splitting hairs for reasons of her own. But Weston was not his concern and Reacher was. He didn't care about her legal balancing act, but he was impressed with the way she slid around the rules without breaking any.

Otto, ever the lawyer, replied, "Understood." Maybe she felt the same way Gaspar did. "We're doing a routine background check on Reacher for the special personnel task force. Anything you can tell us about him would be helpful."

"I looked into the files today when the FBI asked me to preside over Weston's statement and saw that Reacher was here in the late summer of 1997."

A few months after Weston's family was murdered, Gaspar calculated. Also after the killer was arrested and Weston released. About six months after Reacher left the Army, too. He'd failed to get Weston for the murders the first time. His bulldog tenacity must have pulled him back again for another try after his Army discharge, long after he should have moved on.

"I remembered meeting him. He's not the kind of guy you're likely to forget," Carson said. "Weston ended up in Tampa Southern Hospital almost dead that time, too."

"Which explains why Weston didn't attend the first annual memorial service once he was released from jail after his family was killed. And after that, he's been out of the country," Kimball voiced the thought that had occurred simultaneously to Gaspar.

The food was delivered. Carson and Kimball fell on the meal like feral dogs, but Otto ignored her food, focused on Reacher like a heat-seeking missile. Gaspar felt his stomach growling, but felt he should hold back until Otto tucked.

Carson gestured toward the plates. "We don't have a lot of time. We can talk and eat simultaneously. I've done it for years."

Otto lifted her fork and Gaspar dug in as if he hadn't had a decent meal in weeks. Which he hadn't. The food was amazing, even better than he remembered. Exactly the sort of meal his wife loved. The beef was rare and crusted with mango chutney. The Madeira mushroom sauce was light but flavorful. The combination of ripe Bartlett pears, Gorgonzola cheese, candied walnuts and vinaigrette perfectly blended. A dry Cabernet would have made the meal one of his wife's all-time top five. Which meant he couldn't tell her about it. At least, not until he could bring her to experience the meal herself.

"We've never met Reacher," Otto said, barely moving her fork around the ambrosia on her plate. "What's he like?"

"Big. Quiet. No fashion sense at all," Carson laughed. When Otto didn't grin, Carson seemed to consider the question more seriously. Slowly, as if she was uncovering buried artifacts from the depths of memory, she said, "He stood out like a sore thumb, but he exuded confidence like a force field that repelled all challengers. He seemed American, but not American at the same time. In the way that military kids do. Like he held a valid passport but didn't really belong here. He didn't seem to care that he didn't belong. He didn't seem to care about much of anything, actually."

"Was he living in Tampa? Or visiting someone?" Kimball asked. Maybe she was thinking about the gambling situation. Or maybe she thought Reacher was looking for Weston, too.

"He said he was passing through. He asked me where the bus station was. Headed north, I think. Atlanta, maybe?" She wiped the Madeira sauce off her mouth with her napkin and sat back from her plate. "Of course, everywhere in the country is north of here, and most roads lead to Atlanta."

Kimball said, "From what you've described, Reacher doesn't seem like the kind of guy you'd even come into contact with, Judge. Where'd you meet him?"

"Didn't I start with that? Sorry. A fundraiser. We attend dozens of those things. This one was education scholarships for military orphans, I think."

"Where was the event held? At MacDill?"

"Greyhound Lanes," Carson replied. She must have noticed their bewilderment. "Not the bus station or a bowling alley. The dog track."

"Dog racing?"

"Yes. Why?"

"Was Weston there?"

"If he was an officer at MacDill then, he might have attended the fundraiser. Sure. Quite a few military folks were there. It's a big annual event. Very popular. Huge family affair."

Kimball looked toward the two Latin kings across the room. "Anything to do with those guys sitting over there? They look familiar to me, but I can't place them."

Carson turned around to check. "That's Alberto and Franco Vernon. They might have been at the fundraiser. They're not involved with Greyhound Lanes. But they do own a pari-mutuel track a few miles north of here."

"Are they related to Michael Vernon?" Kimball asked, naming the dead man Agent Crane had identified as today's shooter.

Carson set her fork on her plate briefly, composing her reply with care because the question came too close to the case she was handling. "They have a brother named Michael, yes. Theirs is a large local family. Long-time Tampa businesspeople. Significant contributors to the community. Like most large families, some members are more successful than others. But they're protective of their own."

Gaspar received the definite message that no further questions would be entertained about the Vernons. Kimball must have received the same message because she didn't press further. After a few moments, Carson picked up her fork and resumed her meal at a slower pace.

Otto, fixated as ever, asked, "Did Reacher say why he was there? At the fundraiser?"

"If he did, I don't recall. But I'd doubt it. He didn't say much of anything. Not a conversationalist, let's put it that way." Carson glanced at the television mounted on the wall above the bar in the corner. "We're out of time. Let's finish up our food and head back. Agent Crane will report me to the chief judge if we're any later."

The way she grinned made Gaspar feel there was a story there about her relationship with the chief judge she wasn't sharing. Which was too bad. Because it was probably one he'd enjoy.

CHAPTER FOURTEEN

Otto and Gaspar arrived at the hospital's main entrance first. They signed in again at the information desk and wandered through the maze of some administrator's idea of organized healthcare. Eventually, they located the OR waiting room where they had agreed to rejoin the others two hours ago. Nightfall came early in November, but the view from the waiting room window was no less appealing, Gaspar noticed. Bright moonlight and illumination along Bayshore Boulevard rendered it more magical than in daylight, not less.

Agents Crane and Bartos were seated with open briefcases on their laps amid candy bar wrappers and empty paper coffee cups.

"Looks like you guys enjoyed a gourmet supper, too," Gaspar said.

Crane just glowered at him.

"Where's Jennifer Lane?" Gaspar asked.

Bartos replied, "Samantha Weston asked for her about five minutes ago. As soon as Judge Carson and the court reporter get here, we'll all go back in there and finish up and get out of here."

As if his words had conjured her, Carson opened the door and said, "Ms. Chernow texted me on our way back. She says she's setting up. Let's get this done so these patients can get some rest."

They all started after her down the hallway toward the recovery room where they had left both Westons.

After less than twenty feet of progress, everything went to hell.

First, the unmistakable sound of two quick gunshots filled the quiet corridor. A woman screamed. Another woman shouted words Gaspar could not make out. And two more quick gunshots followed.

Otto pulled her Sig Sauer and ran forward, ahead of Gaspar. He pulled his Glock and followed close behind.

Weapons drawn, Crane and Bartos brought up the rear.

Before they reached the room, he heard another gunshot.

Willa Carson ran past them back toward the staircase. An instant later, a horrifically loud buzzing sound exploded around them. She'd pulled the fire alarm. When Gaspar glanced back past the other two agents, he saw the Judge had grabbed her cell phone and was already dialing.

The narrow, hospital-paraphernalia-choked corridor left the agents no choice but to charge single file toward the source of the gunshots.

Just before Otto reached the recovery room doorway, Natalie Chernow dashed out and crashed into her. Otto pushed her against the wall and tried to ask what had happened, but she was sobbing and babbling incomprehensibly. Not that she could've been heard over the alarm in any case, much less over the sirens outside that now joined the cacophony. The din was deafening.

Gaspar supposed he should take comfort in the rapid response rate by everyone involved, but there was no time to appreciate that just then. Otto shoved the court reporter to him and he passed her back to the agents behind him, then followed Otto into the room where he could just hear her shouting "FBI! FBI" over the pandemonium. Sound reverberated through Gaspar's entire body like electroshock.

CHAPTER FIFTEEN

THE FIRST PERSON GASPAR saw was Jennifer Lane.

She stood empty-handed, staring, eyes as wide as basketballs.

The deafening fire alarm continued, now transitioned to incessant blasts brief moments apart, loud enough to wake the morgue.

Just ahead of him, he saw Otto pivot, assume shooter stance and yell, "Hands up! Hands up!"

Steven Kent stood facing Otto, one hand extended with a .38 caliber handgun pointed toward Jennifer Lane.

Slowly, he raised both hands in the air. He pointed the gun in his right hand toward the ceiling. His blue scrubs, face, arms, and hands were splattered with blood. But he made no further move. He said nothing. He seemed to understand what was expected of a man in his situation and he performed appropriately.

Like the pause button on a video had been pushed, all action stopped for a long moment, and then each actor in the drama flew into perfectly scripted motion.

Agents Crane and Bartos quickly controlled the shooter.

Otto confirmed both Westons were dead.

Gaspar approached Jennifer Lane, who stared as if the scene remained paused at a point when Kent had shot both Westons twice in the head, shot and missed Natalie Chernow, and turned the gun on her.

"Ms. Lane," Gaspar said, grasping her elbow. "Jennifer? It's okay. Are you hurt?" She did not answer. Her face was pale. She was breathing rapidly. Pupils were dilated. The skin of her arm was cold and clammy to his touch.

"Come over here," he said, but the accursed fire alarm continued and he had to shout to be heard. He holstered his weapon and tried to lead her away from the carnage, but her terror acted like adhesive on her soles. She would not move.

Gaspar yelled, "Jennifer! Jennifer!"

Finally, she turned her head to look at him, but she didn't see him. He could tell. Grasping her arm again as gently as he could, he again tried to lead her away. But she wouldn't budge.

She returned her stare toward the bloody mess that had been Samantha Weston.

Gaspar tried once more to get through to her. He shook her a little bit and yelled to be heard over the damned obnoxious buzzing of the fire alarm.

"Jennifer! Let's go!" She didn't move.

Then instantly the fire alarm stopped. Its absence was surreal, and the unnerving quiet acted like a switch to release Jenny from horrified rigidity. Before he could do more than slow her descent with his grip on her elbow, she fainted and collapsed into a pile on the shiny waxed floor.

In the eerie silence, Gaspar could hear Crane repeating the familiar words accompanying arrest, including full Miranda warnings. Bartos had collected Kent's gun and was using his cell phone to call for backup.

Otto asked Kent, "Steven what were you thinking? Why did you do this?"

Kent said nothing, which Kent had the presence of mind to know was absolutely the best thing to do under the circumstances.

Agent Crane led Stephen Kent toward the exit.

CHAPTER SIXTEEN

ON THE INSTRUCTIONS OF one of the other agents, Kimball had been standing inside the recovery room blocking the door to prevent anyone from entering. She moved aside for Crane and Bartos to lead Kent away, then pulled the door closed behind them and approached Gaspar.

"Let's get Jenny into the waiting room. We can talk there."

Gaspar saw Otto making use of the small window of calm before the room crawled with crime scene personnel to capture evidence of the murders with her smart phone. She'd find him when she was finished.

For the first time, Gaspar noticed the citrus scent mingling with the metallic odor of blood and disinfectants.

When he looked again at Jenny Lane's pale face, eyes closed, barely breathing in a heap on the polished floor, Gaspar realized why she'd seemed so familiar. She looked ghostly like the victim in a missing person's case he'd assisted for the Tampa FBI detail with some follow up in Miami. The two could have been sisters, even. That victim had disappeared from her home and he'd never heard what happened to her. But her name wasn't Jennifer Lane.

He shrugged. He'd seen look-a-likes before. But he felt better that he'd finally made the memory connection.

Kimball collected Jenny Lane's things from the chair and helped him lift her from the floor. He couldn't carry her. He could barely support his own weight. But with Kimball's help, they were able to move Lane into the corridor.

Agent Bartos stood guard outside the recovery room to secure the crime scene until appropriate crews arrived. In the corridor, the business of a quiet hospital floor between surgeries was returning to normal as hospital security calmed patients and personnel. Soon, a different sort of chaos would ensue as the crime scene was processed.

Gaspar and Otto would escape before then.

CHAPTER SEVENTEEN

THE OR WAITING ROOM would no doubt become command central for the remainder of the night as the scene was processed. For now, the room was available. Gaspar and Kimball half carried, half walked Lane down the hallway.

Willa Carson stood by the door and allowed them to get Jenny settled inside. Ms. Chernow was there composing herself as well.

"Can I have a word with you?" Kimball asked Gaspar. He followed her to a quiet corner. "You're not supposed to be here, are you? Your work is confidential, isn't it?"

He didn't confirm or deny, but her powers of observation hadn't failed her.

"You and Otto should get out while it's still possible. I'll stay here with them and if we find out anything else, I can let you know."

She was right. They needed to go. If Otto didn't show up quickly, they'd be stuck here too long answering too many questions in direct contravention of their orders. The Boss wouldn't like it. But more importantly, he might not be able to erase them from the crime scene once official reporting began.

"Why do you think he did it?" Gaspar asked.

"Why did Kent kill both Westons using the same technique the shooter used to kill Weston's family?" Kimball replied. "Or why did Weston offer himself as a human sacrifice to kill Reacher?"

"Both, I guess."

She shrugged. "Who knows?"

"What's your best guess? That's a place to start."

"The first attack on Weston today was pretty straightforward. Weston was a cat with nine lives. Michael Vernon, the poor dead veteran who tried to kill him, had to be a guy Weston screwed over, like Agent Crane said."

"Makes sense."

"From there, though, it gets tangled. Like I told you, Jenny Lane said Samantha had filed for divorce and offered to testify against her husband to save as much as possible of her assets. Probably a ploy to keep herself out of jail, too."

"Did Lane share any of that testimony with you?" Gaspar asked.

"Not yet. Tangle number two: Weston got a death sentence when he was diagnosed with advanced small cell lung cancer a few weeks ago." Gaspar knew of the cancer, but let her talk. It was almost always a good idea to let people talk themselves out. "Untreatable. He was living on borrowed time. If he'd been conscious when they brought him in here this afternoon, he'd probably have refused those surgeries. It's a miracle he survived them."

"What's your theory on Kent? Why the hell would he do it? Weston was loony enough to hire his own hit just in case Reacher failed to kill him."

"Lung cancer is a nasty way to die," Kimball pointed out. "Weston was a soldier. He would have preferred a quick bullet to the head."

"And then he finds out his wife is about to betray him, so he orders up a two-for-one hit?"

Kimball nodded. "I got about that far down that rabbit hole, myself," she said. "But then—"

"What self-respecting hit man would do his work, then just stand there and let himself be taken into custody?"

Kimball nodded. "Exactly. Not much of a business model. Unless that was part of the deal. Because that's effectively what the first shooter did, too. He left the Weston house, but he was easy to find."

"Or it could have been bad timing. Maybe Kent thought he'd have time to get away and we returned too soon," Gaspar sighed. "Either way, it leaves us nowhere that makes any sense."

"I wish that were true," Kimball said, her mouth had pressed into a grim line. "Because now I'm thinking I dropped the ball."

"How do you figure?"

"I should've remembered."

"Remembered what?"

"Weston's first wife. Meredith Kent Weston. She was Steven Kent's sister."

So it could have gone either way. Vengeance or contract. Gaspar had stopped trying to find logic in criminal behavior long ago. Life wasn't like fiction. Most of the time, he never learned why. Not that it mattered, really. Weston and his wife were just as dead either way.

CHAPTER EIGHTEEN

TAMPA INTERNATIONAL AIRPORT HAD to be one of the easiest airports in the country. Returning the sedan was quick and simple. Security lines were short. For once, they were at the gate without having to run.

Gaspar figured none of this was good news to Otto. She hated flying. The process went better when she didn't have time to change her mind about boarding.

The seats in the gate area were standard black and silver sling seats. Knockoffs of a contemporary design that most normal people had never heard of. All filled with tourists and kids and wrinklies headed in or out of the Sunshine state to avoid winter weather or celebrate Thanksgiving.

Otto seemed unusually preoccupied, even for her. She had her laptop open, her smart phone at her ear. She'd checked in with the Boss. Working. Always working.

She was number one. He was number two. He was only mildly surprised to realize now that he liked it that way.

Gaspar stretched out, folded his hands over his flat stomach, and closed his eyes. He had about thirty minutes to doze. A rare gift.

Otto pushed his arm to wake him up from sweet oblivion ten minutes later.

"What?" he said, not opening his eyes.

"Kimball sent me a file. Take a look," she said.

He glanced over to her laptop screen. Two photos. Each of a brown envelope. One larger than the other.

The larger was hand addressed in block printing to Samantha Weston, c/o Jennifer Lane, Esq. The postmark was Washington, D.C. ten days ago. No return address. Apparently, the large envelope had contained the smaller one.

The smaller envelope looked a little worse for age and wear. Dirty smudges around the edges of a square about the size of a deck of playing cards suggested its contents. Black letters that looked like printing on a police report were placed across the flap to show they were written after the envelope was sealed.

Thomas Weston Recorded Statement

10:04 p.m. 9/1997

The envelope's seal had been broken.

Otto scrolled up the screen to the email from Kimball. The subject line was *Received tonight from J.L.*

Gaspar said, "Kimball said Lane had offered to share Samantha Weston's evidence against her husband. That must be it."

Because Otto would have already noticed, he didn't mention the handwriting on both envelopes looked like Reacher's. They'd seen several examples from his old case files where he printed the same way.

Otto nodded. "Kimball attached an audio file of the contents of the cassette tape in the envelope. I've listened to it. It's a full confession. Definitely from Weston in his own voice. He admits everything Reacher said at the time about how and why Weston's family was killed. And a little bit more."

"Such as?"

"Two big things. He and Samantha were having an affair at the time of the murders. And Weston knew the gang would kill his family, but he put everything in place and then just let it happen. Like a kid choosing to let his dog sleep in the middle of the road, even though he knows he's bound to get run over. He knew they were going to die. He simply didn't know when."

"So you figure Kent found all of this out somehow and that's why he killed them both today when he had the chance?" Gaspar asked.

"I don't have to figure anything. I know he found out today, because Weston told him. Jennifer Lane was right there."

"Weston's plan to get Reacher was a bit more clever than we realized, I guess. He had a Plan B if the suicide by Reacher didn't work at the memorial service." Gaspar resettled himself in his chair and nodded at Otto to go on.

"Weston was defeated," she said. "But he had one last chance. When they loaded him into the ambulance at MacDill, he asked to be transported to Tampa Southern. And he asked for Steven Kent, too. Kent told me it was because he had the necessary clearances. But like you said, what clearances would he need to care for an ex-officer?"

"Weston asked for Kent because he knew him. I can buy that," Gaspar said.

"All Weston had to do was point Kent and let him fire, and make sure Samantha went down with him. He manipulated Kent by telling him what was on that recorded statement and demanding that Jennifer Lane play it."

Gaspar wasn't sure all of this held water, but most of it was plausible. And he didn't want to spend his next twenty minutes arguing with her. Weston wasn't their case. Never had been.

He closed his eyes again. "Good to know. But I never doubted Reacher's evidence against Weston anyway. Did you?"

"That's not the most interesting part though," she replied.

He felt her place one of her earbuds to his ear and turn up the volume on the recording. "This was on the end of the Weston taped confession."

For the first time, relaxed in the Tampa airport, eyes closed, almost asleep, Gaspar heard Reacher speak. It had to be him.

The voice wasn't what he'd expected. Range was higher, for one thing. Tenor, not bass. Speech clipped. Accent sort of nondescript Midwest American. If Gaspar had been pressed to describe it to another officer, he'd have said Reacher sounded less dangerous than he knew him to be. Maybe that's how he got close to his targets.

The words were about what Gaspar had guessed, though.

Reacher said, "You got lucky, Weston. You ever step out of line again your whole miserable life, I'll find you. And I'll make you sorry. Count on it."

Gaspar felt his lips turn up of their own accord as he wondered whether Kent had pulled the trigger on that .38 this afternoon at all.

THE END

I hope you've enjoyed *Fatal Action* as much as I've enjoyed creating it for you. I also hope you'll recommend my books to your friends who might like them, too.

The best way to share your honest review is to post a quick two or three-sentence review telling me what you loved about *Fatal Action* at the retailer where you bought this copy and give the books some stars. Please do that to help me write more of what you want and less of what you don't want. I promise I won't forget! And now that we've found each other, let's keep in touch. Readers like you are the reason I write!

ABOUT THE AUTHOR

Diane Capri is an award-winning *New York Times*, *USA Today*, and worldwide bestselling author. She's a recovering lawyer and snowbird who divides her time between Florida and Michigan. An active member of Mystery Writers of America, Author's Guild, International Thriller Writers, Alliance of Independent Authors, and Sisters in Crime, she loves to hear from readers and is hard at work on her next novel.

Please connect with her online:

http://www.DianeCapri.com
Twitter: http://twitter.com/DianeCapri
Facebook: http://www.facebook.com/Diane.Capri1
http://www.facebook.com/DianeCapriBooks

If you would like to be kept up to date with infrequent email including release dates for Diane Capri books, free offers, gifts, and general information for members only, please sign up for our Diane Capri Crowd mailing list. We don't want to leave you out! Sign up here:

http://dianecapri.com/contact/

CPSIA information can be obtained
at www.ICGtesting.com
Printed in the USA
LVHW030120170821
695429LV00005B/150

9 781942 633662